Ready, Set, Bake!

Ready, Set, Bake!

Coco Simon

Simon Spotlight

New York   London   Toronto   Sydney   New Delhi

SIMON SPOTLIGHT
An imprint of Simon & Schuster Children's Publishing Division
1230 Avenue of the Americas, New York, New York 10020
This Simon Spotlight hardcover edition December 2020
Copyright © 2020 by Simon & Schuster, Inc.
All rights reserved, including the right of reproduction in whole or in part in any form.
SIMON SPOTLIGHT and colophon are registered trademarks of Simon & Schuster, Inc.
Text by Elizabeth Doyle Carey
For information about special discounts for bulk purchases, please contact Simon & Schuster Special Sales at 1-866-506-1949 or business@simonandschuster.com.
Designed by Ciara Gay
The text of this book was set in Bembo Std.
Manufactured in the United States of America 1020 FFG
10 9 8 7 6 5 4 3 2 1
ISBN 978-1-5344-8038-4 (hc)
ISBN 978-1-5344-8037-7 (pbk)
ISBN 978-1-5344-8039-1 (eBook)
Library of Congress Catalog Card Number 2020946005

Chapter One
The New Normal

I woke up this morning feeling totally at peace, even though it was a Monday.

Crazy, right?

But after a few weeks of middle school, I finally felt like I had the hang of things: I knew exactly how long I had to get to each class, where I could hide and take a phone break, and the best locker to grab when I had to change for PE.

One thing I didn't like, though, was that our seats weren't fixed in all our classes. In elementary school, my BFF Casey and I would pick our seats right next to each other on the first day of school, and those would be our seats for the year. We could relax.

Now I'm scrambling to try to get a seat next to

Casey at least half the time. And if we don't time it right, we're way far apart.

I wish I had the hang of that.

Still, I've kind of been loving the routine of middle school. It's funny, because all my life I've dreamed about getting out of Bellgrove, my tiny hometown where everyone knows everyone else's business and routines.

But lately, I've been kind of liking it. I've felt happy knowing exactly where I had to be, what I had to do, and who would be with me every day. For the first time, it actually felt good knowing everyone in town, and having all of them know me. It felt like things were under control.

Speaking of control, my grandmother's kind (but bossy) voice floated up the stairs and curled under my door.

"Lindsay? Sweetheart? Are you up yet? Rise and shine!"

Nans comes over every weekday morning to get me and my younger brother, Skylar, to school. Ever since our mom died two years ago, our whole extended family has helped in different ways to fill the giant Mom-size hole in our lives.

My mom's mom, my grandmother Mimi, is our only relative on her side of the family. Mimi lives in Chicago, but she still tries to visit us as much as she can, and every once in a while, we go to see her. It's really hard on her that my mom is gone, so we comfort each other in both directions.

My dad's family is from Bellgrove and they all settled here. Our family owns a restaurant called the Park View Table, or the Park for short, that's like the hub of our town. It's centrally located and overlooks our beautiful town park, and inside it is a small donut shop called Donut Dreams.

Almost everyone in my family has a job at the restaurant: there's my dad, Mike (he runs Donut Dreams); me (donut counter); my grandpa (manager); Nans (chef); my dad's sister, my aunt Melissa (finances); her girls Kelsey (donut counter with me), Molly (a "runner" or bus girl), and Jenna (waitress); my dad's brother, my uncle Charlie (ordering and inventory); and Charlie's son Rich (waiter) and daughter Lily (hostess).

My aunt Sabrina is a nurse and my uncle Chris is a carpenter who also teaches shop at our town high school, but even they help out at the Park from time to time. We all pitch in together and take care of each other, though lately it's mostly been all of them taking care of me and my family.

All of this has been great for me and Sky and my dad, and I know that. It's just that I really wish my mom were still here. I wish I could have her back, even for a minute, even just to talk about some boring thing in school, or what was going on in her garden.

My mom was an artist, but she was crazy about flowers. She had a beautiful garden out behind our house (it's gotten a little wild, I hate to admit), and she loved planning it and tending it and cutting and arranging its flowers. My mom often said she could have been a florist almost as happily as an artist and art teacher.

"It's the same skill set—shapes and colors!" she used to say.

At the very end of my mom's illness, she told me to remember that after she died, whenever I saw a flower, it would be her saying hi.

And whenever I saw a *blue* flower it would be her sending me a huge hug. Mom's favorite shade of blue was one she used to make using purple, white, and gray paint and she called it "true blue."

It's made me notice flowers a lot more, which I guess was her point.

"Flowers bring joy," she would always say. "Seek out joy!"

But now that fall was settling in, there weren't too many flowers around, and certainly not any blue ones. All I'd been seeing were those tubs with ginormous balls of Halloween-colored mums in them, orange and yellow and rusty red. Yuck.

I missed my mom.

"Lindsay!" Nans called again.

"Coming, Nans!" I whipped off my comforter and scrambled to get ready.

※　※　※　※　※

Downstairs, Skylar was already at the table, eating his bottomless bowl of Coco Snacks, or whatever the flavor of the week was. The kid is always starving, and Nans lets him have junky cereal for breakfast because it's easier to get him out of bed that way.

"Some call it bribery," Nans would sigh when asked. "I call it time management."

My morning job was to get our lunches ready while Nans fixed breakfast. Since our family owns and runs the Park, we're all pretty comfortable in the kitchen.

Nans was making me a quick omelet, just the way I like it with cheddar and chives, while I made ham and cheese sandwiches in whole-grain pita pockets with mustard and baby spinach for me and Sky.

I wrapped them in our new reusable Bee's Wrap waxed cloth (my dad's gone environmental lately as part of some research he's doing for the Park) and filled two small Tupperware tubs with corn chips. Then an apple and a stainless-steel water bottle each, and it all went into our soft, reusable lunch coolers.

I set the coolers by the back door and sat down just as Nans was putting the piping-hot omelet at my place.

"Perfect timing!" she said, kissing me on the head. "Toast?"

"No, thanks," I said as I dug in.

The omelet was delicious—the perfect start to a Monday morning.

"Mmm. Tastes just like fancy restaurant cooking!" I said, grinning. That's a family joke of ours anytime one of us cooks anything.

Nans swatted at me playfully with the dish towel and turned back to the counter to clean up.

"Nans," said Skylar though a mouthful of Coco Snacks. He was already on his third bowl.

"Yes, my love?" said Nans as she scrubbed the frying pan.

"When's it my turn to bring donuts to school for my class? All the kids are asking."

Nans turned off the water and looked at Sky with a smile. "Have you checked the chart?"

Sky shook his head.

Since so many people in the family and in town ask for free donuts all the time, Nans and Grandpa finally had to make a giveaway chart to hang at the Park to keep track of donations.

My aunt Melissa is the accountant at the restaurant and Donut Dreams, and she runs all the finances. She said we'd fall into financial ruin if we didn't keep better track of our donuts.

"You can't keep giving away all your products for free to every bingo night in town! Here are the rules: twice a month, four dozen at a time. That's all we can afford. Tell people to sign up early," she said.

So those are the rules. Each of the seven

grandkids gets a turn to bring donuts to school once a year, and we try to time it with our birthdays. Some families bring cupcakes to school, but we bring donuts. People love it.

The best part is that when it's your turn, you get to go into the restaurant really early in the morning and fill the four boxes with the four dozen donuts in the flavors of your own choice.

My BFF, Casey, is totally down with this tradition and starts reminding me the week leading up to my birthday how much she *loooooves* our cinnamon donuts.

As if I didn't know that by now. As if I wasn't already slotting an entire dozen cinnamon donuts into my birthday assortment way in advance!

Nans continued, "Okay, I'll check the donation calendar for you when I get to work and I'll let you know this afternoon. Your birthday is next month, Sky-baby, so it's coming up!"

Sky grinned, and some gluey chocolate mush oozed through his teeth.

"Ugh!" I groaned, and I brought my dishes to the sink and grabbed my things for school.

Minutes later, we were in the car and on our way.

☀ ☀ ☀ ☀ ☀

Right after our morning meeting, I saw Casey walking toward the lockers.

"Hey!" I said, coming up behind her and pulling on one of her long, dark curls.

"Hey, girl!" Casey said, twirling me around and grabbing me in a hug.

"Long time no talk," I joked, since we try to always text right before we go to sleep and right when we wake up.

We're on a Snapchat streak right now—haven't missed a day in two weeks—and we're trying to keep it that way. We like setting silly goals like that for ourselves.

"I have a big scoop!" said Casey, her dark eyes wide and her eyebrows scrunched way high in excitement.

But before she could fill me in, we were interrupted.

"What's up, chicas?" said my cousin Kelsey, popping open her locker.

She's in my grade, as is her sister, my cousin Molly. They aren't twins, which is confusing since they're almost the exact same age. My aunt and uncle adopted

9

Molly from Korea and then my aunt had a surprise baby, Kelsey.

I liked having them both in my grade—they were so different that they each added a lot in different ways—but we all had our own small friend groups.

"Hey, Kels," I said.

I wanted to hear Casey's news, but I wasn't sure if it was for public consumption. I glanced at her and she looked ready to burst.

"Guess what?" Casey said, looking all around the busy hallway. She lowered her voice to a throaty whisper, and Kelsey and I leaned in. "We're getting a new student today!"

"A new student? Now?" blurted Kelsey loudly, swiveling her head and generally making a Kelsey-like scene. Kelsey doesn't do anything in a small way.

"Shhh!" said Casey. "My mom will kill me if she thinks I'm spilling news."

Casey's mom, Mrs. Peters, is the assistant principal of our school. I love her, since she was my mom's best friend and she's my best friend's mom, but she can be intimidating at school. Very formal-like.

"A boy or a girl?" I asked quietly.

I didn't really need any new friends, so I hoped it

was a boy. A new girl might mean reconfiguring our seating in a class or someone I'd have to—gulp—share Casey with. A new girl would upset my rock-solid middle school routine.

"A girl," said Casey with a grin. "That's all I know!"

My heart sank. How could Casey be happy about this news?

"Where's she from? Why's she starting so late? What's her deal?" Kelsey peppered Casey with questions, but Casey threw her hands in the air and backed away, laughing.

"We'll find out soon enough!" she said.

"If you find out more, will you text me?" said Kelsey.

Kelsey loved our town and was always eager to show people around, maybe even boss them around, if you want to know the truth.

"Yes, I'll text you," agreed Casey. "After school."

We're not allowed to use our phones at school, and Casey's mom is always on the prowl, looking for rule breakers. I'm always looking for spots where I can hide for a minute and watch a video or two, just to relax.

Kelsey sighed dramatically. "Why does everything have to take so long in this life?!"

She spun on her heel and marched off to class, while Casey and I laughed affectionately as she disappeared down the hallway.

"The new girl's in some of our classes," whispered Casey. "That much I do know, 'cause my mom asked me to be nice to her. Let's go!"

We linked arms and set off for study hall and to meet this new mystery girl, but my heart wasn't in it. Our classroom was abuzz as we entered, which was saying a lot for a Monday morning.

What was the deal? Was it because of the new girl?

I scanned the classroom and spotted two big white bakery boxes on Ms. Ogden's desk. They were just like the kind I always used when I had to bring in donuts. There was no other bakery in our town, so what were these and where were they from?

Chapter Two
The New Girl

All the buzzing was definitely about the bakery boxes.

I wondered whose birthday it was. I'd been with the same kids all my life, so I had a good idea when birthday treats were coming up, and I didn't think we were due for one for another few weeks.

I glanced at the birthday chart at the far side of the whiteboard and saw that no one was scheduled until next month.

Huh. And where was there even a bakery near here? Someone must've imported them from Linkstown, about half an hour away.

"Linds! Over here!" called Casey.

She'd snagged two seats side by side. The seat ahead of her was empty but had someone's bag on it.

I crossed the room quickly and rejoined Casey.

As I stowed my bag under my seat, Ms. Ogden turned to face the class, and I could suddenly see there was a new girl with her.

She was petite and had glossy jet-black hair, olive skin, and dark eyes that flashed like she'd just heard a joke. Her ears were pierced and she had little gold earrings that dangled as she looked this way and that, as she smiled broadly at us all. She wore dark-washed skinny jeans with perfectly frayed hems, a floaty, pleated white blouse with lace insets down the arms, and a pair of sleek pink flats on her feet.

"Wow. I bet she didn't buy *that* outfit at the Denim Doll," said Casey under her breath.

The Denim Doll was our local cheap fast-fashion place, with clothes that looked trendy but fell apart after, like, two washes.

I nodded, studying the girl. She didn't seem shy or nervous at all!

If I'd had to stand up in front of a room of new people, my mouth would get totally dry and I wouldn't be able to say a word.

"Class, could I have your attention, please?" Ms. Ogden began with a smile.

The room quieted.

"I'd like to introduce you all to Maria Salas, who has just moved to Bellgrove and will be joining our class. Please join me in welcoming Maria and be sure to be your most helpful Bellgrove selves. Being new is hard!"

Maria laughed, revealing little dimples in her cheeks, and she waved at the class.

"Thanks, Ms. Ogden. It's nice to be here. I've brought some treats to share so please help yourselves. I'm looking forward to meeting everyone."

Treats to share? When it wasn't even her birthday? What was Maria trying to do, bribe us all to like her?

As the class began to buzz again, I watched as Maria made her way through the aisles of desks, returning people's greetings with a smile, and plopped into the seat right in front of Casey.

Casey leaned forward and patted Maria on the shoulder, and Maria turned to her with a grin. Casey whispered something and Maria laughed and whispered something back.

I strained to hear what they were saying, but I couldn't make it out among all the chatter of our class. Casey and Maria said a couple more things to each other, and then Ms. Ogden called us all to order again.

I caught one last thing Maria said to Casey before she turned away: "Thanks for the lunch offer. I'll see you there!"

If I were an emoji right then, I would have been that red-faced mad one. My morning's fears had been confirmed: someone new had entered our class and now things were changing, just when I'd gotten the hang of everything.

Worst of all, what was changing were things between me and Casey, just when we'd finally gotten them sorted out after a couple of weeks of awkwardness.

Casey and I had been a little rocky a few weeks ago, and it was mostly because I was annoyed she'd become this so-called great artist, like, living and breathing her "art," which seemed to kind of come out of nowhere.

Suddenly, she was the expert on photography and sketching and drawing and she was being asked to contribute work to the school website, and I was left in the dust.

And it was my mom who'd been the art teacher

at our school and I was supposed to be the one who was good at art. Only I wasn't that good at it and Casey actually was. This all drove me nuts.

Also, Casey had come home from camp at the end of the summer all stirred up about some boy she'd met there named Matt, and I just didn't get it.

I mean, boys are fine, but who wants to be all lovey-dovey with one? That's just gross to me. Sure, someday I'll probably like one, but right now . . . ugh. No *thanks!*

But Casey was alternating between being all gooey and obsessed with him and then all stormy and not wanting to talk about him, and it was just putting a little rockiness in our otherwise calm friendship.

Finally, my annoyance had grown to the point where we'd had to have a heart-to-heart, and I admitted that her artiness and her boy obsession were pushing me away.

Casey had explained everything then, which made me feel a little better.

The talk made me see that she was still the same old Casey and that her art skills wouldn't make me feel less close to my mom, and her interest in a boy wouldn't make her less close to me.

We cemented our making-up with milkshakes at the Park and a good Snapchat streak.

It had been about two weeks since we'd gotten back to normal, but now Casey was annoying me again with her buddying up to the new girl.

I just didn't think our delicate new balance would be able to stand the weight of someone new joining us at lunch and crashing our friendship. Especially someone who liked bringing yummy baked goods to school.

That was kind of *my* department!

☀ ☀ ☀ ☀ ☀

Mr. Franklin is the art teacher who replaced my mom, and he's extra nice to me. I think he probably feels bad that he got this job because my mom passed away, which makes sense.

A few weeks ago he hung up my line drawing—the kind you create without lifting your pencil—which was an honor. Mine was of my friend Michelle, and it did vaguely look like her.

It was one of my better pieces, but it wasn't exactly good. I felt that maybe he was just looking for any work of mine that was slightly above bad that he could celebrate. Like I said, he's kind, and this makes art class bearable for me, even though I'm missing my mom hard the whole time I'm in his classroom—also known as her old studio.

Today, as we worked on our perspective drawings, which use a vanishing point to make something look far away, I gazed up at my perfectly okay framed line drawing.

Right next to it was a drawing by Casey of our classmate, Riley, running across a playing field. It was pretty awesome, even though it was just a line drawing. It had action and good composition and realistic detail.

It was plain to see: Casey was a much better artist than I was, and she enjoyed it more than I did too.

I looked back at my sketch pad on the table and sighed.

"Come on, Lindsay!" I said out loud, but no one heard me over the din.

Unlike other teachers, Mr. Franklin lets us all talk once he's taught us the lesson for the day. If it gets really loud while we're doing our own work, he'll say, "People, volume, please!" and everyone pipes down.

Anyway, today's chatter was all about Maria Salas,

who was off at some other class right now, probably with Casey, since Casey isn't in my art section either. They were probably already passing notes and playing with each other's hair and making plans for sleepovers.

I was not looking forward to lunch, when I'd have to share Casey with her.

"She's from Chicago!" I heard someone say.

I looked up and it was Melanie Fox, across the table from me.

"The new girl's from Chicago?" I asked, sitting up straight. "For real?"

I adored Chicago, especially because my mom was from there, and I planned to move there one day.

Maybe this Maria and I had more in common than I had expected.

"Yeah! Who'd ever want to move to Bellgrove from Chicago?" said Melanie incredulously.

"Seriously!" I agreed, though inwardly cringing as I realized that was just what my mom had done.

"I would!" said my cousin Kelsey, eavesdropping from another table.

I laughed, since it was so typical of her. Kelsey loves Bellgrove so much that she's barely interested in going away for college.

Ready, Set, Bake!

"We know, Kels!" I called over to her.

"Volume, people!" said Mr. Franklin, without even looking over from the easel where he was working.

"Why did she move here?" I whispered to Melanie.

She shrugged. "I barely had a chance to speak to her. I can't wait for lunch to thank her for those treats. Did you have any of them?"

I shook my head.

Melanie rolled her eyes and said, "OMG, they all looked amazing. Like, cream puffs and little coconut chewies. I had a shortbread cookie with sprinkles, but there were also cookies with frosting . . ."

My mouth watered despite my irritation.

"Wow," I said.

"I wanted to try them all!" said Melanie.

"Not too shabby, Linds," said a voice over my shoulder.

Instinctively, I shielded my paper, but it was only Kelsey.

"Hmm. That's not really a compliment, Kels. Let me see yours," I said.

Kelsey and I can be a little competitive, but we're so different that none of it really matters.

"No way!" laughed Kelsey, darting away from me.

"I'm not part of the artistic dynasty. That's your side of the family!"

I looked up at the other three people at my table, but everyone was suddenly quiet and very, very focused on their work. I knew it was because they were feeling bad for me about my mom right then. Like I said, one of the things that bugs me about Bellgrove is that everyone knows your business. But that can be comforting sometimes too.

Like, I don't mind Kelsey mentioning my mom. It's not like I'm not thinking about my mom all the time anyway. And when people who knew her remember things out loud about her, it kind of comforts me.

Sometimes Kelsey can be insensitive, and that bugs me. But for the most part, I'd always rather have people say things about my mom than not. And the last thing I'd want is for people to forget her.

A quiet voice next to me said, "My mom has one of your mom's flower bouquet cards on our fridge."

It was Jamie Enders, a kid I'd been in school with for my whole life but hadn't spoken to much since the third grade, when we had a weird playdate where he tried to make me eat ants in his sandbox and I had refused to play with him ever again.

"Oh yeah?" I said. "She used to love doing those."

"It's really good," he added. "It looks almost real, and my mom says it cheers her up on rainy days."

He smiled apologetically at me, as if he felt bad mentioning his own, alive mom.

This was one part of grieving I hadn't expected: you end up comforting other people all the time. Whether they're sad about your person who died or they feel awkward not knowing what to say to you, or they worry they should have said something, or shouldn't have said something, it's all just a lot.

My dad reminds me sometimes when I get tired of it that everyone means well, and death makes people awkward. It's good to try to remember that, and like I said, I always appreciate people saying stuff about my mom rather than not.

I smiled back at Jamie. "Thanks. I have one in my room, and there are still a bunch in my mom's studio at home that I like to go look at sometimes."

"Class! Hand in your work and take the last five minutes for free drawing!" Mr. Franklin's voice boomed across the room.

"Want me to bring yours up?" asked Jamie.

"Sure. Thanks."

I tore the sheet out of my sketch pad, wrote my name on the bottom, and handed it to him. It wasn't great, but it wasn't horrible.

I turned back to my sketch pad and began drawing flowers, thinking of my mom's bouquet cards. The Party Shoppe in town had sold them in a spinner rack with a HAND-PAINTED BY LOCAL ARTIST sign on top. After a while, the sign was kind of unnecessary, because everyone knew the bouquet cards were by my mom.

I sketched in a vase under the flowers, and some tendrils and leaves.

Jamie rejoined me and said, "Yeah! Like that, but with lots of color!"

Then he sat back down and we drew quietly, side by side, for the remaining minutes of class.

When the bell rang I said, "See ya, Jamie," and he smiled widely at me.

I guessed we were friends again, ants or no ants.

Now I had to go see if this new Maria girl had taken over my best friend, Casey.

Chapter Three
Friend or Foe?

When the bell rang for lunch, I headed to my locker, stashed my backpack, grabbed my lunch cooler, then looked around for Casey, figuring she'd already be with Maria.

But lo and behold, when Casey arrived at her locker, she was solo.

I looked around her and over her shoulder, but Maria wasn't there.

Had I dodged a bullet? Had Maria found other new friends? I didn't want to mention her for fear of jinxing it.

"Ready?" I asked.

"Yup!" said Casey cheerfully, kicking her locker shut with her foot.

There was a pause as we set off down the hall, and I began to relax.

But then Casey said, "Ria said she'd meet me at lunch."

Not "us," mind you. "Me." *Hmm.* Was Casey planning on ditching me to sit with "Ria" when we got there?

"Ria?" I asked.

Casey nodded. "That's what Maria's friends call her," she explained.

"Oh," I said.

I was quiet while Casey babbled on about long division word problems all the way to the cafeteria.

"I mean, seriously, what do I care when a train leaves Chicago and how fast it's going? I mean, I know *you* probably care, what with your plans to move there and all." Casey laughed. "And Ria probably cares because all her friends are still there."

"Right," I said. I wished I had lots of friends in Chicago.

We entered the cafeteria and I spied our usual table, which was only half-full. Phew. Nothing worse than coming into the cafeteria and having to rethink your plan because your usual spot is unavailable.

I began to cross the room when Casey suddenly said, "Linds. Hold up!"

I turned back and she was waving across the room in the other direction. The person on the other side of her wave was, of course, Ria. She was sitting with a group of girls from study hall.

"Oh, she's all set. Okay, then," I said in relief, turning back toward our table, which had just gained two more people.

There were now only two empty seats left: just perfect for me and Casey. I began to hustle.

"Wait, Lindsay. Ria's waving us over there. Come on!" said Casey.

"But what about our seats?" I protested. "They'll be gone if I don't snag them now. Why don't you go say hi and I'll save the two seats for us?"

"No, we've got to be nice to the new girl. I promised my mom. Plus, she's cool. I want to get to know her! Come on." Casey grabbed my elbow and began pulling me along behind her.

"Casey, okay. Enough. I'm coming! You don't have to drag me!" I shook my arm free and Casey gave me a look.

"What?" I said huffily. "I just don't want to be

dragged like a little kid!" I also didn't want it to look like Casey was making me go say hi to this Ria person, even if that was the truth. It would just look bad.

"Whatevs," said Casey with a shrug, turning away.

I sighed and followed her, feeling like kind of a loser now. As we got closer to Ria, I could see there was a large group of girls surrounding her, and she was showing them images on her phone.

No one seemed to be eating, and I glanced around for the lunch monitor. We weren't supposed to be on our phones at lunch. The school wanted to make sure people ate but also that we didn't turn our brains to mush or do any, like, cyberbullying in the cafeteria.

"Hey, Ria," Casey called.

"Hey, you!" said Ria. She looked back down at her phone. "Oh, here's a good one!" she said, then she handed her phone over to Riley and the rest of the girls leaned in, oohing and aahing.

"What's up, Casey?" said Ria, grinning.

"You all set for lunch?" asked Casey, all smiley and upbeat.

"Yeah! I've got my lunch bag right here," Ria said. "Is it okay if we all sit here together? These girls also asked me to sit with them." She laughed. "My papí was right! Bellgrove *is* the friendliest town in America!"

"We aim to please!" said Casey, swinging her lunch bag onto the table.

Ria was smiling at me. We hadn't actually met yet.

"Hey there!" she said. "I'm Maria. Ria for short."

"Hi, I'm Lindsay," I said quietly.

Ria was so outgoing, it kind of intimidated me, made me quieter.

"Hi, Lindsay. I saw you in study hall. It's nice to finally meet you!"

"Ria, tell us about this one!" said Michelle, interrupting with Ria's phone.

"Are we staying here?" I asked Casey quietly so that everyone else wouldn't hear.

"Yeah?" replied Casey, like, *duh?*

"Okay," I said.

I put my bag on the table and sat down. I had expected Casey to sit next to me, but instead she chose to sit across from me and next to Ria.

I fought back the twinge of annoyance; it was easier for me and Casey to talk if she were across from me anyway.

I unpacked the food I had made for myself this

morning and began to eat while Casey engaged in all the conversation around us.

"Ria, wow! Your family is so talented!" Riley was saying.

"Thanks!" said Ria. "I didn't get any of the talent, though. I'm all thumbs."

I wondered what the talent was that they were talking about.

"Wow! Look at this one!" sighed Michelle. "It's dreamy!"

Ria glanced back at the phone and nodded. "Oh yeah. I loved that one."

I was watching them all while I ate, but I'd be darned if I was going to ask Ria what it was that her family did. But of course, Casey didn't hold back.

"What is everyone staring at?" she said, unwrapping what I knew would be a tuna fish sandwich and taking a bite.

Casey's mom stuck to a strict weekly lunch menu. Would Ria be able to predict what Casey would have in her lunch cooler on any given day? I think not! But I could!

"My family's Instagram for their business," Ria explained.

She hoisted a Japanese lunch box onto the table. It was a small tower of adorable assorted mini food containers in pretty pastel colors, all held together with a wide, hot-pink rubber band.

"Cool lunch box!" Casey squealed, before either of us could ask what Ria's family's business was.

"Thanks," said Ria. "I got it at Rotofugi, this cool Japanese collectible store back in Chicago."

She began to open the compartments and wonderful aromas started drifting across the table.

Everyone turned at the delicious smells and began chattering at once. "Ria! What's in that?! What's this one? What's that one?" they asked.

"My mamí is a really good cook," she answered with a laugh. "This is *arroz con habichuelas*, and these are *empanadillas*. They are all Puerto Rican specialties! I'm originally from Puerto Rico!" she said.

"Wow! You're from another country. That's so glamorous!" sighed Riley.

Ria chuckled. "Actually, Puerto Rico is part of the United States. We're a territory. I bet it becomes an official state soon though."

I had thought the same thing as Riley, and now I was glad I hadn't opened my mouth.

I watched as Ria dug into her food and was super friendly with everyone. She was so confident and breezy, it made me feel like *I* was the new kid and *she* was the queen bee of Bellgrove. This was not a great feeling.

Most of the other girls had to dash off to a yearbook meeting, and soon Ria, Casey, and I were the only ones left at the table.

There were still five minutes left in our lunch period, and while normally lunch felt way too short, today it somehow seemed way too long.

"So tell us about where you're from! Like, how long did you live in Puerto Rico and how long in Chicago?" asked Casey. Her voice was full of excitement.

That annoyed me because Ria was new and exciting. I'm just the same-old, same-old Lindsay, her BFF since the week we were born in the same hospital.

Ria gave us a quick overview, filling us in on her first two years of life in Puerto Rico, then her family's move to Chicago.

"Lindsay has family from Chicago too! And she's always dreamed of living there! Her mom was from there and her grandma still lives there," Casey interjected.

She was only trying to include me in the conversation, I knew, but it annoyed me. Like, I could speak for myself. Plus, I didn't want this new girl knowing all my hopes and dreams on day one.

Ria smiled brightly at me, hinting for me to share more about myself, but I took another bite of apple and fake-smiled through the crunch.

"Does your mom go back all the time? Please tell me yes, since I left behind so many people and things I love!" said Ria.

My heart sank and Casey looked aghast. I usually didn't have to tell people my mom was dead. Everyone in Bellgrove already knew.

Casey put her hand on top of mine and spoke for me. Earlier today, this would have really gotten on my nerves, but suddenly I was grateful for Casey's outgoingness.

"Lindsay's mom passed away a couple of years ago. She was awesome. She was actually the art teacher here."

Ria's eyebrows knit together in sorrow and her brown eyes were warm and sympathetic.

"Oh, no! I'm so sorry, Lindsay. That's terrible. I saw the mural in the hall. Was that for your mom? It's beautiful. She must have been really special."

I nodded and waited for the familiar lump in my throat to appear. I can be fine 90 percent of the time and then one random comment can make me want to bawl my eyes out. But thankfully, today with Ria, it didn't happen.

Casey kept talking, covering for me even though she didn't actually need to. It was nice but a tad annoying all of a sudden.

"Yes, her mom was the best. And she was an amazing artist. Lindsay's also a great artist," she babbled.

"Not really. You're the great artist around here!" I said modestly.

Really?" Ria asked, turning to Casey. "What do you do? Draw? Paint?"

Casey began to chatter on about sketching and photography; she even showed Ria a photo of the portrait she'd recently done of my mom.

"Wow! You're so talented!' said Ria admiringly. "I've got to tell my papí. He's looking for someone local to photograph my parents' work—maybe it could be you!"

"Oh, wow. That would be so cool! What is their work?" asked Casey.

Ria smiled. "It's a cake shop, called the Rich Port Cakery. My parents are kind of cake artists. They make spectacular, arty, themed cakes for special occasions. They're opening a new branch here; that's why we moved. They baked all the things I brought in this morning."

"Is Rich your dad's name?" I asked.

Ria giggled. "No, it's a play on Puerto Rico, which means 'rich port' in Spanish."

"Oh. Right," I said, my face aflame.

Casey covered for me. "A cake shop in Bellgrove! How awesome!" she crowed. Then she looked at me, her eyes shining. "You two have a lot in common!" she added.

I was still embarrassed. "We do?" I asked.

Brilliant, Linds, I thought sarcastically.

Ria smiled at me. "Great! Like what?"

Casey took over again. "Lindsay's family owns the Park View Table restaurant—our number one place to eat in town. And inside, they have the Donut Dreams counter, where they make the most incredible, mouthwatering donuts you've ever tried. You should see the lines in the morning. Right, Linds?" Casey said, giving me a huge smile.

"Right," I agreed.

Her compliments helped me recover from my embarrassment.

But Ria was smacking her forehead now. "Duh! The Park? Donut Dreams? Our families are friends! I think your family is part of why we're here!"

"What?" I asked.

Ria was nodding. "I forget the details, but I'm gonna find out. Our families are friends. That much I know. So now we're friends too! Yay!"

Ria and Casey beamed at me.

I squeaked out a smile and nodded. "Yeah. Friends," I agreed.

But in my heart, what I felt was another story. How could my family possibly be friends with this glamorous stranger who was trying to steal my best friend? One thing was for sure: I would not be fawning over the Rich Port Cakery Instagram like everyone else in my grade. And I needed to get to the bottom of this supposed family friendship.

Chapter Four
Bakery Domination

The rest of the week went by the same way Monday did. All anyone was talking about at school was Ria and her family's new business in town, which was opening soon.

I found out that her grandparents started the Chicago cake shop as a way to give their children more opportunities, just like Nans and Grandpa did for Dad and his siblings, and that her whole family worked there at times.

Rather than making me feel more comfortable around Ria, I thought that the similarities were actually pretty annoying.

How could she and I be alike in any way when we were obviously so different?

Ria was all confidence and friendliness. She chatted with everyone and was cool and at ease in a roomful of strangers (though by Wednesday, all these strangers had become her friends).

I was reserved and shy—attributes that my mom had always called "thoughtful" and "serene," but maybe that was just her being nice and putting a positive spin on things, as usual.

I wasn't sure thoughtfulness and serenity were such great qualities anymore—not when I watched Ria zipping around, chatting up and charming everyone.

Even the lunch ladies were calling her by name by day three. Pizzazz and confidence seemed to pay off better than thoughtfulness and serenity.

What's more, Ria had totally taken over with Casey during the week. They were hanging hard: after school, and with weekend plans and everything.

Yes, it's true that they invited me every single time. But I had things to do! I couldn't just go hang out at the drop of a hat like some people apparently could.

I was hoping that all Casey's socializing would come back to bite her when we had a math test on Thursday.

But no, she and Ria had studied together on

Wednesday (I had declined the invitation to join them), and it turned out they both aced the test when we got it back on Friday.

I didn't do as well as they did.

What's worse: Casey broke our Snapchat streak.

She apologized like crazy, and normally I wouldn't have cared. But having it come on top of this Ria friendship explosion made it that much worse.

Then Ria invited me and Casey to sleep over at her house on Friday, but I legitimately had to study for an English test after working at Donut Dreams, so I said no thanks.

Casey agreed, though, and my heart sank.

"If anything changes, please come, Lindsay," Ria had said, and she sounded sincere. "My mamí really wants to meet you, especially now that she knows you're part of the Cooper family."

I'd managed to ask my dad about the Salas family and their connection to our family only briefly this week, since he'd been really busy with getting ready for a conference presentation and negotiating to buy some new coffee equipment for Donut Dreams.

When I asked him, he was racing to get Skylar to soccer and said something like, "Oh yeah! Those guys are so nice! I need to have them over for dinner . . . ," and then he was gone.

Though he'd confirmed the connection, I wouldn't exactly say it sounded like we were friends with them, which made me feel better. I was satisfied that Ria had inflated the relationship in her mind, and, judging by my dad's breezy response, that dinner wouldn't be happening anytime soon.

It was always better to have other people think you were better friends than you actually were, better than thinking it yourself about them, for sure.

※　※　※　※　※

By the time Friday rolled around, I was ready for a big break from Ria and the Casey-Ria lovefest. Again, Ria was nothing but nice, but her confidence, her big-city background, and news of her family's "cakestagram" were all just wearing on me.

At lunch, I'd still sit with her and Casey, at Ria's table but I had to listen to their endless chatter about photography and memes and what would be a great cake shot for Instagram.

To include me, Casey started pressing me on why Donut Dreams didn't have an Instagram account. She knew perfectly well that Kelsey begged my grandpa all the time for a Donut Dreams Insta account, but he thought social media was the downfall of civilization and always refused.

Yet discussing all this in front of Ria made my family seem ignorant and behind the times. I was tired of it all.

The bottom line was, I was looking forward to hanging with my family and forgetting about Ria Salas for a couple of days.

After school on Friday, I got home, dashed upstairs to change into my Donut Dreams "Dream Team" T-shirt and ditch my book bag, then had a quick granola bar (if I don't eat before my shift, I start sneaking in donuts) and tied my hair back, per Grandpa's work rules.

The afternoon was dreary and I had a couple of minutes to spare before my Donut Dreams shift. My mom's bouquet cards had been on my mind all week, ever since Jamie had brought them up in art class, so I decided to visit her studio before I headed out.

My dad's been working in my mom's studio more lately, but I try not to go in there too much. I feel like every time someone besides her enters it, a little more of her escapes or what's left of her energy gets diluted. I mostly save my visits for when I'm really down or missing her.

Today wasn't like that, though. I was aggravated about Ria and Casey, for sure, but I was more curious about my mom's work today than anything else.

I clicked on the lights and inhaled the scents of linseed oil, paint, dried herbs and flowers from the hanging bouquets around the room, and a certain Mom smell—maybe it was roses, from the Portrait of a Lady perfume she always wore. It still smelled the same as ever, and just breathing deeply made me feel good.

I walked straight to the far wall, where she had a clothesline strung up for displaying works in progress.

The line was hung with sketches of people, mostly me and Skylar and my dad. They were already pretty out of date—Sky especially had changed in looks since Mom died. The line on the wall opposite the portraits had ten of her bouquet cards clipped to it—some she had already colored, while others were just line drawings. I moved closer and studied them.

Mr. Franklin always talked about filling the page with your work, and that's what my mom always did with these bouquet cards. They were "generous," as she used to say—bursting off the edges, bursting with color, bursting with life and energy. Beautiful, just like she'd been.

I turned away and tried not to miss her so much. As I moved around the room, my eye traveled and caught on certain things.

My mom's bucket of paintbrushes, a shelf jammed with cleaned glass jars for her flowerbombs (surprise gifts of flowers she used to make for friends), a tray of small watercolor pans, the cornflower blue worktable that my dad had had my uncle Mike paint for her a few birthdays ago as a surprise.

She had loved it. It wasn't Mom's favorite "true blue" color, but it was the next best thing.

Next to her table was a small bookcase filled with a mixture of titles. One whole shelf had huge thick books about famous artists, many about Claude Monet, her favorite painter. Another shelf had some art technique books and museum guides, and two other entire shelves were filled with books about flowers and gardening.

I pulled out a thick illustrated book called *The Encyclopedia of North American Flowers* and set it on the table. I flipped randomly through the glossy pages and the book fell open to a marked page. It was cornflowers, or *Centaurea cyanus* in Latin.

Blue flowers.

My mom was sending me a hug.

Tears pricked my eyes and my throat closed up with a lump. I fought the urge to cry my eyes out.

"Hi, Mom," I whispered back, smiling a little through my tears.

I closed the book and smoothed my hand across the cover, then gazed out the wall of windows to her garden in the back.

"Your garden is looking a little neglected," I whispered. "Especially at this time of year."

I went to put the book back on the shelf, but then changed my mind and tucked it under my arm instead. I wanted to spend a little more time with it, but for now, I had to go.

I clicked off the lights and pulled the studio door shut behind me. I placed the book on the coffee table in the TV room and headed off to work. I was looking forward to poring over the book when I got home tonight.

※　※　※　※　※

Ready, Set, Bake!

Kelsey was already in place behind the counter when I arrived. Her dad must've dropped her off on the way to take Molly to soccer, because there was no way Kelsey would be early if left to her own devices.

In the back, I hung up my coat and washed my hands, and I was still tying my apron on my way back out when the Friday after-school rush hit.

Suddenly, where there'd been no customers moments earlier, there was a line of hungry teenagers. They all wanted hot drinks, and many of them wanted donuts.

Kelsey and I got to work.

I must've served twenty cups of hot chocolate and ten flavored teas, not to mention around thirty donuts, by the time the rush passed. There were still a bunch of older kids hanging out at the little tables in Donut Dreams, and our area behind the counter was trashed.

When Kelsey and I rush, we don't really clean as we go. This makes us faster, but it drives Grandpa crazy if he sees it. Now we had to move into high gear to get it all cleaned up before he did his pre-dinner lap.

Grandpa does "laps" of the Park all day long—up front, all around the tables, into the kitchen, around the front of Donut Dreams, and behind the counter. He bends down, looks underneath stuff, slides his finger across surfaces, you name it.

I could see him beginning a lap at the far end of the restaurant. That meant Kelsey and I had about four minutes to whip this place into shape before he got here.

"He's lapping," I said to Kelsey in an urgent whisper.

Her eyebrows rose and she sped up her rinsing in the sink.

"How long do we have?" she asked.

"Three and a half minutes," I replied. "Go!"

The thing about selling donuts is that the toppings and crumbs get everywhere. There were rainbow sprinkles on the glass case top, mini chocolate chips on the floor, streusel crumbs littering the table tops, tiny M&Ms on the coffee fixings table, and more.

I dashed out and began wiping the empty tables and removing discarded cups and napkins. I'd need to get a sweeping in, and Kelsey had to refill the milks and sugars on the fixings table too.

I squatted down to get an eye-level view of the tables, because that was how Grandpa always checked them, and I realized I was using a sponge that was leaving greasy streak marks. Now I had to wipe everything again.

I chucked the sponge in the garbage and went behind the counter to get a new one just as Grandpa headed into the kitchen.

"Two minutes," I said to Kelsey.

"On it!" she said, hustling the milk jugs behind the counter to refill them from milk cartons in the fridge.

I rushed to clean the tables and fixings counter, and I was just turning back to go change the sponge for the broom when some movement outside the plate-glass restaurant window caught my eye.

It was Casey and Ria, walking their bikes slowly up the sidewalk outside. Casey had her overnight bag in her bike basket, and they were obviously on the way to their sleepover.

I stood there with my jaw hanging open, watching as my best friend made a new best friend without me.

"Lindsay!" said Kelsey in a sharp reprimand. "What are you doing! He's coming!"

I snapped out of my daze to see Kelsey looking at me, but then I turned to look out the window again and Kelsey's eyes followed mine.

"Oh!" she said.

Just then, Casey turned and saw us and waved, a huge smile on her face.

Ria also started waving.

Kelsey spun away, ducking into the back to see if there were any donuts left to refill the emptied display trays.

But I couldn't do anything. I just stood there until I heard Grandpa's voice behind me.

"Are we selling statues at Donut Dreams today?" he joked.

I turned around and began to move again, his voice giving me a surge of adrenaline.

Inside I was chanting, "Please don't come in, please don't come in," because if Casey and Ria arrived and I had to wait on them, I'd just about keel over at this point.

"That's my girl!" said Grandpa as I swiftly grabbed the broom from its peg on the wall and returned to begin sweeping the floor of the seating area.

I snuck a glance outside and thankfully, the twosome was gone.

Grandpa inspected the tables, squatting as usual for an eye-level view. Then he went to the fixings counter and lifted the milk jugs to make sure they were full, peeked into the sugar packet bins for the same reason, then came around to look at the display case and the back side of the counter area.

He was nodding the whole time, which was a huge relief.

Kelsey and I exchanged a glance, acknowledging that the inspection was almost over and we'd be okay.

But then, at the last second, Grandpa found a flaw.

"Girls, there are coffee grounds all spilled back here. Coffee's expensive. We can't go throwing it around, plus it makes a real mess if it gets tracked. Clean this up, please."

Darn it!

I hadn't seen the coffee grounds—the countertop in the back is black, and I hadn't squatted down to check it at eye level.

Grandpa moved away to look for trash outside the front of the building—always his last stop on his laps—and Kelsey and I breathed a sigh of relief.

"That wasn't too bad," she said. "Right?"

I nodded, but now my mind was back on Casey and Ria and their sleepover.

"So what's up with your BFF hanging with the

enemy?" said Kelsey, her head cocked to the side.

Kelsey is my cousin and I love her, but she's also in my class in school, works with me, and attends every family event that I do. She's always in my business and right now, I just didn't want to drill down into it with her.

I shrugged it off.

"Casey's mom asked her to be nice to the new girl, so I guess that's what she's doing. They did invite me," I added awkwardly. It sounded pathetic when I said it out loud.

"Right, well anyway"—she sniffed and tossed her ponytail—"you shouldn't be hanging with the enemy."

"Wait, she's the enemy because . . . ?"

Kelsey's eyes flashed. "Duh! Because they're here to open a bakery, selling sweets and coffee just like us. They'll be direct competition for the Park and Donut Dreams. Come on!"

"Wait, what? I thought they only made cakes, like fancy decorated ones for weddings and bar mitzvahs. I didn't realize. . . . What else do they sell? Will they have tables and everything, or just takeout?"

"Who cares? It's going to eat into our business no

matter what! And it's all Grandpa's fault!" she added.

But then she clapped her hand over her mouth like she'd just blurted something she shouldn't have (which was a classic Kelsey move).

"Why?" I asked.

But Kelsey kept her hand over her mouth and shook her head, her eyes wide.

"Come on, Kels," I said. "If you know, then why can't I know?"

"Because you'll say something to your dad and it will come back to bite me, like everything does!" she said, grinning.

I growled at her and threatened her with my broom, but she whirled away, laughing.

"Want to come to the movies after work with me and Sophia and Riley?" she asked.

This was a very kind invitation, but I didn't need her pity and anyway, I was tired. I was truly looking forward to going home, showering, getting into my pajamas, and looking at my mom's flower book.

"Thanks, Kels. That's really nice, but I'll take a rain check."

"You sure?"

I nodded.

Plus, I really needed a break from thinking about Ria Salas, and I was sure that was all Kelsey and her friends would want to talk about.

Now I just had to think of a way to find out more about the Salas family's plans for Bellgrove bakery domination.

Chapter Five
Baking Science

When my dad got home and saw me in my pajamas by seven o'clock, he declared it a PJ Night, and he and Skylar went to put theirs on too.

By seven thirty, we were all in pajamas, eating Uncle Mike's chili out of bowls on our laps in front of the TV in the den. "Tastes just like fancy restaurant cooking!" we all chanted when we sat down to eat it.

My mom never let us eat anything outside the kitchen, but my dad has bent this rule, saying we can do it if he's with us, since we're growing up and more careful now.

It was really cozy. We each had our own seat—I had the couch, with Nans and Grandpa's dog Fred nestled in next to me (he basically lives with us now)—and we each had our own cozy throw blanket to cover us.

Sky had had three bowls of chili, and now he and Dad were playing some horrible video game together while I looked at the flower book, and at eight thirty we were going to watch a movie and Dad would make popcorn.

PJ Night and Popcorn and Movie Night are two of the things my dad has started in the past couple of years. He decided we needed some happy new traditions that weren't Mom traditions; we needed to "seek out joy" as a new family unit, and it has really helped.

We also have Field Day, where we skip school one day every spring and do volunteer work, and we've done a long weekend in Chicago every year so far. Dad's open to new suggestions too.

The flower encyclopedia was amazing. How had I never looked at it before? It had so many kinds of flowers, with so many beautiful color pictures. I recognized a lot of the names and a lot of the flowers in the pictures, but I wouldn't have been able to put them together before this.

There were a few chapters at the back on planning

and tending flower beds, and it got me thinking.

"Dad?" I asked.

"I got you!" he shouted at Sky, and they both fell backward screaming and laughing.

I rolled my eyes. "Dad?" I tried again.

"Yes, sweetheart?" He turned and gave me his full attention.

"What are you thinking for Mom's flower beds?" I asked.

"Umm . . . I'm not really thinking anything?" he answered honestly.

I smiled. "Are you planning to keep them going?"

"Well, yes! Of course. Why?"

I shook my head a little. "Just wondering. I was looking out at them today and thinking they looked a little sad and lonely."

He tipped his head to the side and studied me, and I could tell he was a little worried.

"*I'm* not sad and lonely, Dad!" I laughed. "I've just been thinking about flowers a lot lately, and . . . I don't know. I think they're kinda cool. It seems like a shame to let all of Mom's hard work disappear, you know?"

Dad smiled. "Well, first of all, I'm glad you're not sad and lonely," he said.

Then he folded his hands over his knees and looked thoughtful. "I do want to keep up your mom's garden. I really like it, and I loved it when she used to do those flowerbombs."

Somehow the word "bomb" penetrated Sky's video-game daze and he turned back from the TV to look at us with a grin, his thumb still tapping over his controller.

"Those were cool! We should do those again!" he exclaimed.

Dad and I smiled back, remembering Mom's many flower surprises and people's reactions. Sometimes we'd hide to watch what happened when people got them. It was like something from that TV show, *Funniest Home Videos*.

"Yeah, I agree," I said. "But the garden has around six or seven months until we can start cutting flowers again. I was just wondering if we should be tending it in the meantime. Like, it says something in here about winter mulch?" I shrugged.

"Good idea," agreed Dad. "Let's take a look at it tomorrow and see what needs doing. In the meantime, maybe look online for any tips. We should definitely take care of Mom's garden."

"Rematch?" asked Skylar.

"Nah, I'm all video-gamed out, kiddo. I'm going to make the popcorn. You guys get the movie set up and then we'll watch, okay?"

He gathered our empty chili bowls, and while Sky got the movie up on Netflix, I scrolled around on my phone to see what was up.

Among many other Snaps, I had a message from Casey (*now* she remembered!) and Ria, saying they missed me and wished I hadn't had to work.

"Well, *I* wish you two weren't turning into best friends," I muttered.

"What?" said Sky, turning to me.

Oops. Had I said that out loud?

"Nothing, thanks," I said.

I opened my browser and thumbed through some pages on winterizing your flower beds.

When my dad returned, I had the beginnings of a plan for the garden.

The popcorn was steaming in a big bowl, and my dad gave us each a cereal bowl to fill with our own serving.

Sky pressed play on the remote and put on an old movie from the 80s about a boy who makes a wish and suddenly turns into an adult. It's kind of silly, but it's a feel-good movie, so we all love it. We recite a lot of the lines along with it.

As the first scene unfolded, I turned to my dad. "All we need to do is weed the garden, give it a good watering, and put some mulch on it. Then we need to make a plan for any replanting in the spring."

"Perfect," said my dad. "We'll do it Sunday after Sky's soccer," he said, and we all settled in to enjoy the movie for the twentieth time.

※　※　※　※　※

Unfortunately, the weekend ended up being a rainy washout, so we didn't get to work on the garden. My dad promised we'd do it the following weekend instead.

But it was okay because we had a big Cooper family dinner at the Park on Sunday night, and it had been a while since we'd done that. Everyone had been trapped indoors all day doing homework, so dinner was high energy and fun, with all the cousins and aunts and uncles there.

We played charades at the end, and Grandpa stumped us all by trying to act out what an emoji was. He got so frustrated that we were all laughing hysterically, even Nans.

Later that night I was scrolling through Instagram after my shower, only to find five posts from Casey about all the fun and wacky things she and Ria had done at their sleepover, including photos of a big fancy cake they'd made with help from her parents.

My blood boiled, and I tossed and turned until I fell into a fitful sleep, with nightmares of Ria and Casey leaving me behind time after time.

And then, as if I hadn't had enough of Ria Salas, my science teacher announced a new team project first thing Monday morning and made Ria my partner. Ria and I would have to develop a project together that illustrated some aspect of chemistry.

After the teams were announced, the whole class had to reshuffle our seating. I knew I should be gracious and make the first move to go sit with Ria, but I was grumpy and just not in the mood. The longer it took for our partnership to start, the better.

But Ria hustled over to my desk with a big smile, and when my classmate Carmen vacated her seat next to me, Ria nabbed it and dragged the stool toward me.

"Casey's going to be so jealous that we're together!" she said with a grin.

She busied herself sorting her things onto the desktop and stowing her bag underneath the desk.

"Yeah," I agreed mildly.

I wasn't trying to be cold, but I also wasn't going to be super hyper and make her think I was happy about this pairing.

She popped back up and was still smiling. "So. Chemistry, huh?"

"Yeah," I said.

I felt awkward being one-on-one with Ria. I suddenly realized that Casey was usually with us, running interference, babbling away, meeting Ria's energy with her own. It was easy for me to fade into the background and let them do all the work, but now I couldn't hide.

Ria took a deep breath and seemed to calm down all of a sudden.

"Do you like science?" she asked quietly.

"Yes," I said. "Um, do you?"

Making small talk with new people was not something I often did alone. For all my talk about moving away from small-town Bellgrove, I suddenly realized I'd have to improve my social skills if I was going to make new friends anywhere.

Ria nodded. "Yes. I like how it's often like math, but then there are cool real-world applications for it. Last year I started helping out more at my family's cake shop, and there's a lot of chemistry in baking."

Uh-oh. We were getting on a tricky topic suddenly.

"I know," I said cautiously, not wanting to talk about her cake shop at all.

"People don't realize it, but, you know, the amount of activators that you use in your recipe can totally change the taste, the height, the density of the crumb. It's crazy!"

"Right!" I agreed.

But to myself I was thinking, *Um, activators?* I'd heard Nans using all these terms before, but I wasn't totally sure what they were.

I gulped. Did Ria think I had more to do with making the food at the Park and Donut Dreams than I actually did?

"Maybe we should do something about food science for our research project. That would make sense for the two of us foodies, right?" she suggested.

Actually, it *was* kind of a cool idea. And we

certainly did have that in common. I sat up a little straighter in my seat.

"Okay," I said, feeling a little more energized. "And maybe we could, like, bring in samples for our presentation!"

Ria laughed. "Yes! Woo them with sweets. Works every time!"

We both laughed. It was actually kind of cool to meet someone whose family had the same experiences as mine.

"The upsides of being in the food business are pretty good. Like family dinners with great cooking, birthday treats that rock . . ." I started ticking things off on my fingers.

"Totally!" agreed Ria. "People at my old school looked forward to my birthday cake every year. It was a running joke, and people would take bets on what flavor and theme it would be." She looked wistful.

"When's your birthday?" I asked.

"Oh, it was in September. So not for a good long while again."

"Well, maybe you can think of another reason to bring in a cake this year. Like, Groundhog Day?"

We both giggled.

"May Day?" she suggested.

"Saint Patrick's Day?" I added.

"Puerto Rican Day!" she crowed. "Hey, that's actually not a bad idea, come to think of it. There really should be a Puerto Rican Day!"

"Ooh, that would be perfect. What would you bring?" I asked.

"Well, the traditional flavors of Puerto Rico are—"

"Lindsay and Ria! How is the project topic planning coming along?" Mrs. Baldeschi called from her desk at the front of the room.

Ria and I both blushed and ducked our heads, caught for chatting rather than working.

Mrs. Baldeschi winked and shook her pencil at us. "I need a topic and a possible thesis by the end of the period, girls. Please get to work."

"Oops," said Ria quietly.

"Busted!" I joked.

We smiled at each other, partners in crime.

"Okay, so testing activators . . . ," I began.

"Right. Maybe we should narrow it down, like to leavening agents," Ria said.

I was embarrassed. I didn't want to have to admit

I didn't know what those were. "And that would be ... between ..."

"Well, all kinds of things can make baked goods rise, but yeast is kind of a hassle, because there's a waiting period, you know? How about between baking soda and baking powder?" suggested Ria. "Instant gratification. So similar and yet so different."

"Right!" I agreed hastily to cover my ignorance. "So perfect."

"And so easy to test," added Ria. "Let's think of a thesis."

"Hmm." I thought about it. "Maybe, which one produces a better cookie?"

A cookie seemed neutral enough. It wasn't my specialty (donuts) or Ria's specialty (cakes), so it was good common ground.

"Yes. Perfect," agreed Ria. Then she sighed happily. "It's really nice to have a friend whose family is in the same business as mine," she said. "I've never had that before."

I smiled. "Me neither. Most of my friends have no idea about all the gross stuff I have to do, like wiping down sticky tables, taking out the garbage, hosing down the floor mats. . . ."

"Oh, I know! Sometimes little kids smear frosting all over the tables, and it gets so disgusting," Ria said with a shudder.

"Girls!" warned Mrs. Baldeschi.

We straightened our faces but our eyes were dancing merrily. It was kind of mean of me, but I was pleased to think that Ria and I had this bond that Casey couldn't have with her.

"So funny," murmured Ria.

"Okay, should I be the note taker?" I asked, taking out a fresh sheet of paper to write down our topic and potential thesis.

"Yes, please. Let's say our topic is 'Leavening Agents in Baking: Differences and Similarities.' How does that sound?" said Ria, back to serious school mode.

I nodded as I copied it down.

"Great," I said. "And for our thesis? How about something like, 'Baking powder and baking soda have different chemical properties that create different results in baked goods. Which one makes a better cookie?'"

"Yes. Perfect," agreed Ria.

I wrote it down with a flourish and added our

names to the sheet. Then I showed it to her for her approval.

Ria nodded. "This will be fun," she said.

I was surprised to find myself agreeing with her. "Totally. I'll bring it up to Mrs. Baldeschi now," I said, smiling.

We had a few minutes to kill before the end of class, and Mrs. Baldeschi told me that we could chat quietly now, as long as we didn't bother anyone else.

"What was your favorite birthday cake you ever had?" I asked Ria.

Her eyes got a dreamy, faraway look. "Oh, that's easy. It was a chocolate cake with pale pink cream-cheese frosting, and fresh pink roses all over it. It was so beautiful, like a ballerina's tutu come to life. You can see it on our cakestagram, from last September. It's so pretty."

"Okay," I agreed. I'd avoided their account for so long, but I guessed I'd have to look now. "Do you guys use flowers a lot when you're baking?"

Ria nodded. "My mom, especially, loves to put fresh flowers on our cakes as decoration. And sometimes she puts edible flowers on them too. She likes a lot of flowers." She laughed. "I mean, the woman is crazy about flowers," she added.

"Same. I mean, my mom was too. She'd probably have liked your mom's cakes," I offered.

"Right, and your mom did a lot of art with flowers, right? That's what Casey told me, and I saw some stuff in the mural."

I nodded, then searched for that familiar lump in my throat but again, it wasn't there. I wondered why it didn't feel so bad to talk about my mom with Ria.

"Yeah. She loved flowers."

Ria smiled. "They probably would have been friends, our moms," she said.

"Yes," I said. "They probably would have."

"I'm sorry she died," said Ria.

"Thanks," I said, wondering again why it wasn't as sad to talk to Ria about my mom as it was to talk to Casey about her.

And then the bell rang and we both went off to our next classes with a smile and a wave, while I was left wondering if I'd just been a traitor to my family by making friends with the "enemy."

Chapter Six
Bellgrove Bake-Off

I didn't have to wonder for long, as it turned out. At around five o'clock, I spotted Ria walking into the Park View Table with what appeared to be her parents and a little brother.

Kelsey stopped in her tracks. "Some nerve!" she said in a low, angry voice.

I felt a surge of adrenaline—my palms felt kind of sweaty all of a sudden, and my heart was beating hard. Was there going to be a showdown? How would I handle it if so, now that Ria and I were kind of friends?

My older cousins were clueless—they didn't know who the Salas family were or the threat they posed to our livelihood. Lily greeted them warmly and seated them. Jenna brought them menus.

But Molly knew. She started over with a pitcher of water to fill their glasses, and then she stopped, a scowl on her face. She'd obviously just realized who they were. She looked around to see if my grandpa was anywhere near, watching. Then she set down the pitcher and went on break in the back.

"OMG, did you see what Molly just did?" I asked Kelsey.

Kelsey folded her arms and narrowed her eyes as she watched Jenna chat with the Salas family.

"She did the right thing. Unlike some people." She shook her head as she watched Jenna.

But suddenly, something shocking happened.

Grandpa and Nans came out of the kitchen and headed straight for the Salas table, their arms outstretched in welcome and huge smiles on their faces.

All of the Salas family stood up.

"Coop! Jane!" cried Ria's dad.

"Pete! Serena!" my grandpa was saying.

And then, something even more shocking happened. Grandpa and Nans joined the Salas family at their table! This had never, *ever* happened before, despite customers constantly inviting my grandparents to sit with them.

Grandpa called sitting with customers "a slippery slope." He'd always say, "Once you do it for one of them, you've got to do it for all of them, or people's feelings get hurt. And if I'm sitting in a booth all day, who's gonna run the place?" His policy was to sit with family only, and even then it was rare.

"Oh my gosh!" sputtered Kelsey. "No way!" She clearly had the same shock as I did.

We stood and watched as my grandparents settled in, chatting and laughing happily with Ria's parents. Jenna brought over more menus, and Molly skulked out of the kitchen and picked up the water pitcher to fill all the water glasses while giving everyone a suspicious side-eye.

Ria greeted Molly warmly—I knew they were in a few classes together—but Molly just smiled a closed-lip smile and nodded at her, then hurried away.

My aunt Melissa came out of the office just then and spotted me and Kelsey standing there doing nothing.

"Girls? Nothing to do? I could give you a few jobs!"

We snapped back to reality.

"No, Mom. We're fine. We've got stuff to do," Kelsey said firmly.

I wished my own mom were here to give me the scoop, but Aunt Melissa was the next best thing.

"Aunt Mel, what's the deal with the Salas family? Aren't they, like, our enemies or something?" I whispered.

"Enemies?!" Aunt Melissa threw her head back and laughed. "Just the opposite! Grandpa is very good friends with Mr. Salas."

"What? Seriously? Come on, Mom," said Kelsey.

"For real," said Aunt Melissa. "They met, oh, probably ten years ago at a trade show. They were on a panel together and they hit it off.

"Grandpa would visit them and their cake shop once in a while in Chicago. And Nans has gone in with him and had dinner with them as a couple. They're really nice people.

"Wait, isn't the daughter around your age? Maria?"

My jaw was on the floor, but I closed it and nodded. "Yes, she goes by Ria. She's in our grade."

"But Mom, wait. Aren't they opening some new bakery here with coffee and tables and treats, and it's going to ruin our whole business?" Kelsey asked.

Aunt Melissa just laughed. "Where do you get these crazy notions, Kelsey?"

Kelsey said, "Well, I overhead you and Dad talking and I just assumed—"

Aunt Melissa's face darkened. "Kelsey Jane Lakes, you are not to eavesdrop. If I ever find you doing that again, there will be serious consequences."

But her face relaxed a bit as she continued. "Now, you might have heard me say the Salases are opening a bakery, and you might have imagined the part about it being bad for us.

"In fact, it's going to be great for us. Coop's been trying to get them to move out here for years. Not only because he knew they'd love it—it's such a great place to raise a family, after all—but also because we're going to combine all our ordering with theirs and save a fortune."

"Wait, what?" asked Kelsey, dumbfounded.

Aunt Mel nodded. "Ingredients and supplies are expensive, and in this business, the big guys get all kinds of breaks because they order quantities in bulk. Now that the Salases are here, ordering in bulk will help both of our businesses out."

"But aren't you worried about their bakery eating into our profits?"

Aunt Melissa just laughed. "Not at all. They're not going to serve cooked meals, and that's where we make all our money. Our donuts and coffee are a nice perk—haha—but they're not our bread and butter. Sorry for all the food puns. Plus, this town needs a good bakery desperately.

"And anyway, they specialize in Puerto Rican sweets—it will be all new and different, stuff you've never tried or even heard of before; nothing like what we offer. You'll see."

I felt an enormous rush of relief. I'd been starting to like Ria, and it would not be convenient for me if she really was the enemy.

But Kelsey was still skeptical. "Yes, we *will* see," she said darkly.

Aunt Mel shook her head and laughed again, then went over to say hi to the Salas family.

Kelsey took the opportunity to take her phone out of her apron pocket.

We are totally not allowed to use our phones when we're working, and it made me nervous that Kelsey was doing so now.

"Kels!" I cautioned. "Remember, Grandpa has eyes in the back of his head!"

"Shh! They're all busy!"

Have I mentioned that Kelsey is not exactly the queen of impulse control?

"What are you doing?" I asked.

"I just wanted to see if there are any photos of the new bakery yet."

The storefront of the Salas bakery had been wrapped in brown paper for months, and everyone in town had been speculating on what kind of business it would be.

I had been hoping it would be a bookstore, but even once I knew it was going to be a cake shop—or bakery, rather—I had no idea what to expect.

"Oh, look," said Kelsey, holding her phone out to me.

I pressed her arm so it was hidden under the counter. If my grandpa ever looked over and saw us both on a phone while we were on duty, he'd go nuts.

Cautiously, I glanced down. It was a photo of the front windows of the store, and they'd put up the lettering on the glass.

RICH PORT CAKERY, it said in blocky gold letters

with red trim. It looked really cool, actually. You couldn't really see anything inside, since this photo was all about the windows.

"Wow! Nice!" I said, looking up again to make sure I wasn't busted.

"But look who took the photo," said Kelsey wryly.

I snuck a glance back down and read the caption. *Photo credit. Casey Peters.* My stomach lurched.

"Traitor," said Kelsey.

"Hmm," I said.

I was confused. On the one hand, the Salas family were quite obviously not the Cooper family's enemies. One look at Nans and Grandpa laughing it up with the Salases across the restaurant made that quite clear.

Also, I was warming up to Ria. She'd been nice in science—I liked that more mellow side of her—and I was looking forward to working on our baking project together. It was relaxing being with someone who understood my family's business.

But I didn't like Ria and Casey being so tight. That was still true.

I sighed and began the process of cleaning up. It was almost closing time for Donut Dreams, and the final half hour of my shift was always dead. Not a lot of people eat donuts or drink coffee after five thirty p.m.

Kelsey continued to stalk their Insta feed.

"Mmm, the Salases bake a lot of interesting stuff. At the new bakery, they're going to have something called flan, and something called *quesitos*. I guess those must be the Puerto Rican specialties my mom was talking about."

"Oh," I said, emptying the coffee grounds into the trash.

"Ooh, look at this! Wow!" said Kelsey, taking full advantage of Grandpa's preoccupation to openly flick through her phone.

I glanced over at what she was showing me on her screen. There was a photo of a giant white cake totally covered in masses of fresh flowers, all rainbow colored.

"Oh, that's so pretty!" I said. "It reminds me of . . ."

"A flowerbomb! Just like your mom used to send. And guess what? That's what the caption says! Can you believe it?"

"Oh, that's so funny, Ria said her mom loves flowers, just like mine. Funny they used the same term for it. What are the chances?"

Kelsey held the phone out to me. "When Casey Peters is the one writing the caption, the chances are pretty high. This is from only two days ago."

"Oh. Wow," I said.

I couldn't help it: I felt betrayed.

Not by Ria, obviously, because how would she even know? But by Casey. I felt like she'd taken something that was precious to me and just given it away.

Kelsey was watching me. She can be protective of me, but it can sometimes get a little out of control.

I didn't want her to get all mad at Casey. It would not serve any of us well. I swallowed my anger and feelings of betrayal.

"I'll speak to Casey about that," I said quietly.

"You better!" said Kelsey.

※　　※　　※　　※　　※

We had totally cleaned up the Donut Dreams area and I was just starting to remove the trays of remaining donuts from the cases to put in the kitchen while Kelsey took out the trash (it was her turn).

Every night my grandpa boxes up the leftover donuts and hangs them in a bag on the back door of the restaurant. The people from the food pantry in the next town over come to pick them up after hours to serve in the morning.

The donuts still taste great the next day—especially if you warm them a little bit—but Grandpa will only serve super fresh donuts here at Donut Dreams, so Nans makes new batches every day.

Grandpa likes to brag about "Zero waste!" at the Park, and food donations are part of that policy.

Kelsey had wheeled the big garbage can out the back door to ditch the trash when I heard my name.

It was Ria and her family, standing at the edge of Donut Dreams.

"Oh, hey, Ria!" I said.

I left the trays behind and quickly rinsed my hands, then went around the counter to say hi.

"We didn't want to come over and bother you. We can see you're closed," she began. "My mom is just dying to meet you because she's heard so much about you. And Kelsey, too. Mamí, this is Lindsay Cooper. Lindsay, this is my mother, and my dad, and my brother, Luis."

"Hi, everybody! Nice to meet you all. Welcome to Bellgrove."

I used my friendliest Park View Table manners. My grandpa would have been proud, but Kelsey would probably have been mad that I was speaking to them at all.

"Oh, Lindsay, we're so happy to meet you!" said Mrs. Salas, who was friendly and warm, with bright eyes, curly dark hair, and very red lipstick. "We've heard so much about you from your grandparents, and from Maria. I'm so happy you girls are in class together."

"Thanks. Me too," I said. "What grade are you in?" I asked Luis.

He was tiny, with a dark crew cut and an Iron Man T-shirt.

"Second," he said. "But I'm turning eight soon."

"Ooh, I'll bet you have a great birthday treat in mind for school," I said. "Maybe something with a superhero theme, I'm guessing?"

He grinned. "Yup!"

"You know it!" said his dad, ruffling Luis's hair.

Ria's dad was handsome, with thick black hair and dark eyebrows above flashing eyes and bright white teeth. Both of Ria's parents had a big-city sheen to them.

I felt a little intimidated, even though they were friendly.

"Can I tempt any of you with a donut?" I asked. That's what Grandpa always says: "tempt you." It just came out naturally.

Mr. and Mrs. Salas protested that they were too full, but Ria and Luis each wanted to try one, so I beckoned them over to the case so they could choose.

It took Luis only one second. "Could I please have the Oreo crumble one?" he asked, his eyes huge.

"Coming right up!" I said, putting the donut on a paper plate and then sliding it into a bag with some extra napkins. "You don't have to eat it all at once, you know. You can save half for breakfast."

I leaned over to whisper to him, "That way, if Ria eats hers all tonight, you can show off that you have half left at breakfast!"

Luis began to laugh. "Thank you! Mamí! I have a funny idea!" he called, and he returned to his parents.

Ria was laughing. "Thanks a lot!" she joked.

"I have a little brother too. I know the drill. Now, what kind can I give you?" I asked.

"Um, could I please try a glazed?"

Glazed? I was a little disappointed. That's, like,

our original flavor. I wanted to show off a little and highlight a better choice, something really creative.

I bit my tongue though because I just didn't know Ria well enough to make her change her choice.

Just then Kelsey arrived back from trash duty and watched as I used a piece of bakery paper to put two glazed donuts in a bag for Ria. I figured I'd make up for the plainness of her choice by giving her two.

"Hi, Kelsey," said Ria, all smiles.

"Hey, Ria," said Kelsey, kind of cool. "You're getting a glazed?"

Ria looked at her and then at me uncertainly.

"Should I not?" she asked.

"No, no, glazed is good. I promise. Here you go!" I said, sliding the bag to her.

Kelsey was looking at the bag disdainfully.

"It's just that there are so many fun flavors to try. Glazed is kind of . . . basic."

That was Kelsey's way of saying "boring," and Ria caught her drift.

"Oh. I'm sorry!" Ria said, her eyes wide. "I should've . . . it's just . . . well, I felt like I'd really get to taste the donut, you know? I can try the other kinds later, once I know what the actual donuts taste like."

I glared at Kelsey. She was being mean for no reason.

"I like the glazed too. Don't worry. There will be plenty of time to try all our flavors."

One minute ago I'd been annoyed at Ria for picking our most boring flavor. Now I was defending her? I was confusing even myself.

"You should try them warmed up in the microwave. Just ten seconds. You'll love them," I added generously.

"Thanks," said Ria, but she seemed a little deflated.

"Hey, and I'll find out if my grandma uses baking powder or baking soda for the donut batter!" I offered, trying to cheer her up. "Or maybe it's yeast?"

"Who's giving away my baking secrets?" said Nans, appearing from the kitchen door.

We all laughed.

"Speaking of which, I just had a brilliant idea to bring more awareness to the Rich Port Cakery," said Nans. "Come!"

She beckoned us over to where Luis and Mr. and Mrs. Salas were speaking with Grandpa at the front door.

Kelsey, Ria, and I followed. I couldn't imagine

why Nans felt like the Salases needed more attention for their bakery. It seemed to be all anyone was talking about these days. (Or posting about on Instagram!)

I remembered Casey's posts and got a little jealous all over again.

"I've decided we should have a Bellgrove bake-off!" Nans said proudly to the group. "It's been a long time since we've had a new place to eat in this town, and it will help people learn all about the new bakery!"

The Salas family were overjoyed, but I was (once again) shocked. Why would my grandparents think this was a good idea? What if the Salases won the bake-off? Would anyone still want to come to Donut Dreams if we were the losers?

We said our goodbyes amid a lot of chatter, and then Grandpa closed the front door with a smile that quickly faded as he looked at Kelsey.

"Don't let me see you on your phone in Donut Dreams again, Kelsey Jane, or I'm docking your pay."

He went over to Donut Dreams to bring the remaining trays into the kitchen for boxing.

"But . . . how . . . ????" For once Kelsey was at a loss for words.

"Eyes in the back of his head," I hissed after he walked away.

"Oh, shush!" said Kelsey crossly. "Start thinking of some brilliant donut flavors for the bake-off, you traitor!" she said bossily.

"On it," I agreed, ignoring her peeved tone. "And we should also start working on Grandpa again to do an Instagram account for Donut Dreams. Only I don't think it should be you who asks him. Maybe Jenna or Lily. Or Molly, or even Rich. Heck, even Sky could ask instead of you," I added, naming all the other cousins.

"Go home!" said Kelsey crossly, but she wasn't serious.

"So long!" I called.

Then I hung up my apron and darted out to meet Dad and Skylar in the car outside. I couldn't wait to speak to my dad and get some clarity on whether the Salases were our friends or not.

Chapter Seven
Honesty

Skylar was eating a huge half of a turkey sandwich in the back seat when I got into the car.

"Hey, Sky," I said, shutting the car door and buckling my seat belt. "Dad, I need your opinion."

Dad eased the car out of the restaurant parking lot. He chuckled. "Those words are music to my ears. What's up?"

I turned in my seat to face him. "Are we supposed to be friends with the Salas family? Like, what should I do about being science partners in school with their daughter? Are they going to take all our business away? That's what Kelsey says. And why is Casey helping them? I feel like our friendship is dead. And what's up with this bake-off idea? Is Nans crazy to do this? What if it hurts us? And how's it going to work, anyway? I mean . . ."

"Whoa! Slow down! You've got ten different topics going here. Start over and go one by one."

I took a deep breath and explained everything to him. It felt good to get it all laid out at once, finally.

My dad thought for a second and then he began.

"Okay, I don't know anything about a bake-off. Let's start with the Salas family. I had a chance to ask Grandpa about them and his history with them. He told me . . ."

Dad went on to say pretty much what my aunt Melissa had said earlier. Friends for a long time, combining ordering, yada yada. He agreed with Aunt Mel that their bakery would not eat into our profits at Donut Dreams.

"People who like donuts, like donuts," he said. "Most people will go to both places for different reasons. Now, as for being science partners with their daughter: Is she nice?"

"Actually, she is," I admitted. "I like her, but I wasn't really sure we should be friends, because of our competing businesses. Kelsey says she's the enemy. And I don't like that she's taking over Casey. On the other hand, it's nice to be friends with someone in kind of the same business as us."

"Hmm. Well, you should definitely be friends with her then. What's her name?"

"Ria," I said. "Short for Maria."

"You can't help what Kelsey thinks right now, but make up your own mind about Ria. Don't hold other people's grudges. The Salas family is really nice and not our enemy.

"And as for Casey, I'm in a little over my head when it comes to middle school girls' friendships. That might be one for Nans. All I can say is, you and Casey have been best friends your whole life, and that counts for a lot. If she's upsetting you, you need to tell her," Dad said.

I sighed. "I don't know. It's awkward."

We pulled into the driveway and Dad turned off the car.

"Give us a sec, Skylar, okay?" Dad said.

Sky got out, still chewing, and headed inside, while Dad and I stayed where we were.

Dad turned to face me. "Lindsay, it's best to be direct in life. Asking questions so you have the facts and telling people straight up how you feel is the only way to go. Anything less than the truth causes problems that are unnecessary, and they only grow the longer you leave them."

"That's kind of a guy attitude," I said. "It's not really how girls work."

He smiled at me. "Don't be sexist. It's a human attitude. And it's a recipe for success. Just have a heart-to-heart with Casey. Be. Direct. Call her when you get inside. You won't regret it. Now tell me about this bake-off."

I did not like the idea of calling Casey, but I pretended to go along with it. Then I explained Nans's idea and Dad chuckled and shook his head as I spoke.

"You've gotta hand it to her. She's a mover and shaker," he said.

"Do you think it's a good idea? I mean, what if we lose?"

Dad laughed. "I think Nans is too smart to set up a competition where anyone would lose. She'll come up with something that showcases everyone's strengths, just like she and Grandpa do at the restaurant. You'll see."

I sighed. "I guess."

He rubbed my shoulder. "Don't stress so much, kiddo. Everything's going to be okay. Okay?"

"Okay," I said.

"And we'll work on Mom's garden this weekend, too. That's something to look forward to."

I opened the car door, "Good. Thanks, Dad."

"Come on in, now. I've got a nice turkey sandwich for you, and you've got homework to do, and calling Casey."

Upstairs in my room, I looked at my phone.

Did I really need to call Casey? No one called anyone anymore. She might think it was an emergency. Plus, it's so much easier to hide your feelings behind Snaps and photos and emojis and TTYLs.

I smiled, thinking of Melanie and her abbreviations, then I set my phone aside. I'd call later, after dinner and homework, for sure.

Then dinner and homework passed, and I did not call Casey.

When my dad came to tuck me in and asked what she'd said, I mumbled something about not reaching her. It wasn't a lie! I hadn't reached her.

Dad made me promise to address it the next day and I did.

Tomorrow was so far away, anyway.

But now it was today and Casey was right near my locker, joking with some other girls.

"Hey, Linds!" she called across the hall, but she didn't come over to see me like usual, and her eyes were kind of cool and guarded.

It was sort of a test, I thought. Like, was I going to go say hi to her or was she going to have to come over to me?

I just nodded and waved back, and I felt worse for it as I walked to class alone.

At lunchtime, I wasn't sure what to do. Casey had been inviting Ria to sit with us every day, so I assumed that was her plan today.

But when I got to the cafeteria, Casey was standing by the door alone.

Was she waiting for me?

"Hey," I said cautiously.

"Hey," she said. She seemed to be waiting for me to make the first move.

"Are you waiting for Ria?" I asked.

Casey shook her head.

I took a deep breath before I asked, "Want to sit together?"

She released a deep breath she'd been holding. "Yes!" she said.

We crossed the room to our usual table and set down our lunch coolers.

"Chicken salad on rye?" I asked.

It was Tuesday, after all.

She smiled. "You know it. What are you having?"

"Pasta salad."

This small talk was kind of awkward, but it was better than nothing, I guessed. I wanted to ask where Ria was, but I didn't want to jinx myself. If Casey said Ria was on her way or something, I'd have been really upset.

We opened our lunches and got all set up, all without a word, which was highly unusual. It felt like we didn't really know each other that well, which was a feeling I didn't like at all.

Then, we spoke at the exact same second!

"Casey, I—"

"Listen, Lindsay—"

We laughed.

"You first," she said.

"Okay." I took a deep breath and thought about my dad's advice before I said, "My dad and I were talking about being honest and direct, so I just wanted you to know I feel hurt that you and Ria are becoming best friends, and I'm sad you shared 'flowerbombing' with the Salas family."

Casey's eyebrows rose all the way up and her eyes were immediately sympathetic.

"Oh my gosh, Lindsay, flowerbombing! I'm so sorry! I never even thought of it. I just think your mom is so cool and I wanted to share some of that coolness and maybe make it seem like it was my coolness too. I never thought it would upset you. It was more like a tribute. You know?"

I noticed that Casey was talking about my mom in the present tense, as if she were still alive, which made me soften a little.

"Well, it made me sad, is all. There are things of my mom's that I just kind of want to save for myself, you know?"

Casey was nodding miserably.

"I'll take it down. I promise. I never should have used it in the first place," she said sadly.

"No, don't take it down. It's fine. It's just, I think it's all tied into my feeling weird about your friendship with"—I lowered my voice—"Ria. And it's extra awkward for me because, like, her family is starting this thing that might be bad for my family."

"Wait, I thought your families were friends," said Casey. "I'm confused."

"Well, yes, they are. But it doesn't really make sense to me. I keep wondering how Donut Dreams and the Rich Port Cakery can coexist in such a small town."

"Oh," said Casey. "I never thought of that. They're so different."

"I mean, my dad and Nans and Grandpa aren't worried. Neither is Aunt Mel. In fact, our families are co-hosting a town bake-off or something, to launch the Salases' bakery."

Casey's eyes lit up. "Cool! Can anyone enter?"

I smiled. "I'm not sure. Nans is going to figure the whole thing out. You know her."

Casey rolled her eyes. "Do I ever. I'm sure it will be done with military precision!" she laughed.

"Like an invasion!" I started to laugh also.

"It will be perfect. That's for sure," said Casey, shaking her head in admiration.

I felt a warm surge of love for her right then. I loved that she admired my mom and my grandmother, and that she knew them so well. That kind of friendship was irreplaceable. I couldn't let it go. I had to fight for it! And that meant being honest.

"So, I just wanted to say, about"—I whispered again—"Ria." Then I resumed my normal voice. "I think she's nice also. It just hurts my feelings that you're like, helping launch their business and it might be a threat to ours!"

"Oh, no! I never even thought of that. It was just really, selfishly, a way for me to showcase my photos. I know you think I'm annoying with my art, but it's something I've really gotten into, and I want to keep going with it," Casey said. "Maybe social media isn't the best route, especially if it's hurting your family. I don't have to help them. I can start a new account of my own and post there."

"No, you don't have to stop! I just wanted you to know. And I don't think your art is annoying. It just seemed to come out of nowhere and also, as you know, I feel bad I'm not a great artist like my mom. And you are.

"So I'm kind of jealous—it's silly, but I am. Just like I'm jealous that you want to spend all your time with her now," I said.

"But we invite you every single time!" Casey pointed out. "And I thought you'd love to be friends with her, since she's from the big city, unlike boring old me—"

"You're not boring!" I interrupted. "Who says you're boring?"

"Well, I mean, we've been friends our whole lives and we're from the same place, and our families are all friends, and like, my sister and your cousin Jenna are friends, and I don't really bring anything fresh to the table.

"Plus, Ria's fun! I know you'd like her if you give her a chance. You just get so shy when she's around. And she wants to be your friend. She's always mentioning you when I'm with her, and how your families are such great friends, and how she hopes you'll give her a chance," Casey said.

"Whoa! Wait a minute. Okay." I stopped eating my pasta salad and took a sip of water. "First of all, you are not boring at all. You are fun and smart and talented and cool and we always have fun together. Plus, you're a great friend in bad times, too. As for her, I feel sort of intimidated, I guess. She's got a big personality and she's from the city.

"And she seems like she's taking all your attention. I feel like I'm the boring one around here, if anything," I finished.

"No way. Never," said Casey. "You're not boring at all. And I don't think she's too 'big cityish.' She never brags about it or anything."

"She must hate it here!" I said.

"No, she loves it. Her parents are a lot more available, and she loves being in a house instead of an apartment. But you should find this all out for yourself. From her! Why don't you say yes the next time she invites you over?"

"I don't know. Maybe," I said.

"And why don't you and I make a plan to do something this weekend. Just the two of us. K?"

"K," I agreed, smiling inwardly. "And hey, we have to start up our Snapchat streak again."

"Totes," agreed Casey. "I realized I messed that up, and I'm sorry. Then I remembered Friday and did that one with Ria, but I couldn't send you the private one later to start up our own streak again. My phone died that night and Mrs. Salas made us charge them downstairs so we wouldn't be up all night on our phones."

"Sounds familiar," I laughed.

Casey's mom always does the same thing. She thinks that phones on sleepovers are too much of a temptation and that bad things usually come of letting kids have their phones at night. From stories I've heard, she's probably right, even though Casey gets mortified by this rule.

"I know, right? At least I'm not alone."

"You're never alone," I joked. "You've got me!"

"Thanks, dude," said Casey with a grin. "Now what should we do this weekend?"

"I'm free Saturday night! Want to sleep over?"

"Totally."

After we finished eating, Casey headed to the library to grab a book she needed, and I went to my locker to relax with my phone for a minute.

But I was surprised by the message that awaited me. It was from Ria. It said:

> Hey can you sleep over on Saturday? We could work on our project! LMK!

Chapter Eight
Garden of Friends

Nans was at home when I got back from school, which was a relief.

I don't like to burden my dad with too much stuff, but Nans is always like, *Bring it on!* Plus, she's a girl too (sorry to be sexist, Dad), so there are things she just gets. I needed her advice on a lot of stuff.

"Hey, sweet girl!" Nans said as I came in.

Skylar was at the table, eating a massive roast beef sandwich.

"Where do you put it all?" I asked him.

He just looked at me blankly as his jaw worked an oversize bite he'd just taken.

"Would you like me to make you a sandwich too?" Nan asked, winking at me.

I dumped my book bag on the floor. "No thanks. I'm just going to have some iced tea."

"Okay. But I do have a few of these cinnamon buns I've been fooling around with for the bake-off," she said temptingly.

She opened a Tupperware container on the counter and showed them to me and Skylar. They were golden brown swirled with dark brown cinnamon, with thick white icing poured across their tops and down their sides.

"Um, I changed my mind. I think I need one of those right now, please." I went to the sink to wash my hands.

"Thought so!" Nans singsonged. She got a spatula and lifted a bun onto a plate for me. "Warmed?" she asked.

"Well, if you insist," I joked.

She microwaved it for twenty seconds and handed the plate to me, along with a knife and fork.

"You'll need these. They get very gooey when they're warm."

"Oh, bummer," I joked again.

I sat down at the table and cut a bite and put it in my mouth. The texture was incredible—crisp on the outermost layer, warm and chewy inside, with the tangy sweetness of the frosting and the spicy warmth of the cinnamon laced through every bite. I groaned.

"Nans, these are amazing! OMG!"

I took another bite, then another. Soon the bun was gone. I licked my lips and scraped an extra bit of frosting off the plate with the side of my fork, then ate that, too.

"Wow. You are totally winning the bake-off with those things!" I declared.

"They are pretty good, right?" Nans asked, smiling. "I'll leave the rest here for breakfast tomorrow."

Skylar was putting his now empty plate in the dishwasher. "You promised, right?" he said to Nans.

"A deal's a deal. But I get to check your homework first, and it has to be perfect!"

Skylar said, "Deal!" and he took off for his room, scooping up his knapsack on the way.

I looked at Nans. "What's the deal?"

She rolled her eyes. "He has a huge project due for social studies and some other homework. I gave him a big snack to get his energy up, and I told him if he finishes by the time I need to leave for the restaurant, he can watch a show."

"Nice," I said. "Good deal."

I lingered at the table, wanting to spill everything to my grandmother but unsure where to begin.

"How's Casey?" she asked.

I looked up. "Dad told you?"

I wasn't mad. It made it easier, actually.

She shrugged. "He just mentioned in passing that things were a little awkward between you two. Some stuff to do with Maria?"

I sighed. Then I explained everything to her, including Casey's work on the cakestagram, her using "flowerbombing," her friendship with Ria, my worries about the Salas bakery opening, our talk, the sleepover dilemma, everything.

Nans asked good questions, and after about fifteen minutes, I felt like she was totally caught up.

She'd come to join me at the table and now she laid her hands on it, palms down.

"Okay. There are two things going on here, and then they overlap in the middle." She put one palm overlapping the other halfway. "On the one hand is your friendship with Casey, which is going through some changes right now. On the other hand is the arrival of Maria and her family. And the overlap is where Casey and Maria are becoming friends and Casey is doing work for the Salases' Instagram."

"Right," I agreed.

"So I think you need to have this sleepover with Casey this weekend. It's really important that you carve out the time to nurture your existing friendships, especially the one that means the most to you. You can tell Maria you'll work with her in the afternoon, and then have Casey come over at six. You and Casey need to keep the open dialogue going and also make sure to have some fun, so it's not all a drag."

Nans went on. "Now, I don't mean to be the bearer of bad news, but friendship is a two-way street. You might be doing stuff that bugs Casey, or she might just want some time away from you. Have you considered that?"

I'd been feeling like such a victim that I hadn't really thought of that.

"Why? Do you think maybe I'm a bummer to her because of my mom?"

Nans raised her eyebrows. "I wouldn't put it that way, but it could be hard for her, too. She adored your mom and misses her a lot. I know that from her mom, who also really misses your mom. So being over here or with you could be sad for her. Also, she might worry about you, and that's a heavy load for a kid too."

I thought of how Casey had used the "flowerbomb" term on the cakestagram in honor of my mom, and also how she had jumped in to explain about my mom to Ria at lunch the first day.

"Yeah. True."

"As for Maria—"

"Ria," I corrected her.

Nans smiled and continued, "I think you are naturally thoughtful and selective when making new friends. You always have been, and that will serve you well one day when you move to a big city. You can't just become buddy-buddy immediately with every person you meet."

I liked how Nans said "when" and not "if" I move to a big city. I also liked how—like my mom—she always spun my shyness as a plus rather than a minus.

"Ria does seem like a lovely girl, and Coop and I really do adore her parents. We've known them for a decade, so give her a chance. Go ahead and see if it works for you two to be friends. Don't feel pressured by us, though. You need to make up your own mind. She doesn't have to be your best friend either. Just a new friend. That's always nice to have," Nans said.

She had a good point. I could be friends with Ria without making her and me and Casey into the Three Musketeers.

Nans slid her palms along each other.

"The friction—the tricky part—is where your feelings about Ria and Casey rub together. You feel possessive and threatened and all those things that make us human. It's totally natural. I suspect that as things improve with each of the girls, this friction will settle down. There's room for all of you to be friends together and separately, all in your own ways. And never mind about the Rich Port Cakery threatening the Park.

"Cross my heart—there is no threat to our livelihood. In fact, besides the ordering advantages for us, a new bakery could help make our town become more of a foodie destination, which could only be good for us. Right?"

Hmm. That was a good point too. "Okay," I said.

"Anyway, you need to let the grown-ups worry about those kinds of things. You can't worry about everything! Leave something for the rest of us!" She leaned over and grabbed my hand and gave it a squeeze.

I smiled. "Thanks, Nans."

"Now, in other news, your dad told me you'd like to take care of your mom's garden. I think that's a wonderful plan. I'd love to help you, but I do not have a green thumb at all. But someone we know must. I'm sure we can get you some advice."

"Okay. Well, I found some info in her books and online, so we can at least get started."

She nodded thoughtfully. "You know, if you think like a gardener about your problems, it all kind of makes sense. Look at it this way: you've got a garden you're growing, right? And you have some deeply rooted flowers in there that you love. They're reliable and you're used to them. That's Casey. Now, an opportunity comes along to add a new plant to the garden: that's Ria. You might love it, or just like it, or maybe not like it at all in the end. But wouldn't you rather try it out?"

"Hmm," I said. I thought I knew what she was saying.

"Would you rather have a very orderly garden with only a couple of plants and nothing out of place, in strict rows, pruned to death, never changing? Or would you rather have one bursting with life and color, with new surprises, different plants in the mix, with new colors and fragrances?"

"The mix, definitely."

Nans beamed, happy that I understood her metaphor.

"Same with your mom. She loved having new plants to add and clippings from friends to grow. And yes, sometimes she removed plants that weren't working, but I don't think you're there right now. Just plant these new seeds in your friendship garden— while tending the plants you already love—and see how it all turns out. Okay?"

"Okay," I agreed.

"Good girl." Nans stood and kissed the top of my head. "Now I'd better go make sure someone's working on social studies and not Fortnite. I'll be right back."

"Thanks, Nans."

"Love you, sweetheart."

☀ ☀ ☀ ☀ ☀

I liked Nans's idea of my "garden of friends," and it helped me think about Ria and Casey in a different way. Both friendships needed some fertilizing and attention. The Casey one so it could keep growing strong, and the Ria one to see if it might take root.

That night, as I did some research on garden care after my homework was done, I realized what a good comparison Nans had used. Gardens needed to be protected from frost (just like friendships), gardens needed to be fed (just like friendships), gardens needed weeds taken out as soon as they appeared, and the plants needed to get along with each other, in order for everything to flourish.

I texted Ria to say that I could hang out Saturday afternoon, but that I already had plans for Saturday night.

She wrote right back to say great and could I come meet her at the bakery so we could use some of the supplies there for our project.

My palms began to sweat at the idea of being on "enemy" territory, but I brushed away that thought. Maybe it would be better to just get it over with; at least I wouldn't keep wondering about their bakery and what they'd be serving.

Without overthinking it, I texted back to say yes and that I would see her at noon.

With that done, I texted Casey to confirm our sleepover.

I didn't have to work on Sunday morning, so we could sleep in and then, after she went home, I could work with my dad on the garden, and head over to the bake-off, which would be on Sunday afternoon.

It was shaping up to be a good weekend.

Meanwhile, plans for the bake-off were falling into place. In her usual style, Nans had enlisted the whole town to participate, it seemed. She had also decided the bake-off should be a fundraiser to help homeless children, so the bake-off was now also a bake sale, with a small competition component open to twenty bakers.

Nans had had my cousin Rich create a SignUpGenius account so that people could register for the event to say what they were baking. The bake-off slots filled up quickly, and I was looking forward to sampling all the goodies.

The panel of judges would be made up of local authorities, including Casey's mom and the mayor and some other important grown-ups around town. The whole event would be held Sunday in the town park, across from the Park restaurant, and the town was paying for a big white tent—just like in *The Great British Baking Show*—in case of rain. The mayor was having local bands play throughout the afternoon.

If it all went well, the town was considering making it an annual event. (Have I mentioned that my town loves annual traditions?)

Skylar and I went to the Park after school on Wednesday because Nans was wrapped up in recipe testing and couldn't get over to our house to supervise our after-school time.

I dropped my book bag at a sunny booth in the corner, then headed into the kitchen with Sky to scrounge up a snack.

In the kitchen, Nans was standing at her baking table, an apron cinched around her waist, her whiteish-blonde hair clipped up, and flour everywhere—even on her nose. There were bowls, pans, measuring cups, muffin trays, ingredients, mixers—everything all over the place, like someone had turned the kitchen upside down.

"Hey, kiddos!" she said, a little distracted.

"Nans! What is all this? What are you making?" I asked.

She looked around. "Well, I'm making my grandmother's Russian sable cookies, my mother-in-law's caramel fudge, the cinnamon buns you tried yesterday, pumpkin muffins with maple frosting, let's see. . . ."

"Nans! That's a lot!"

"But what about donuts?" asked Sky. "Aren't you going to have donuts in the bake-off?"

Nans looked at him blankly. "What?"

"Aren't you going to do donuts for the bake-off?" he asked again.

"Well, I wasn't thinking so," said Nans. "No."

"Wait, what?" Sky was surprised. "Why not? That's what we're known for!"

"I just figured we should wow everyone with something new."

Skylar grabbed a spoon to snag a lump of caramel fudge and hopped up on a stool to eat the sweet. "Nope."

"How many things can you submit for the competition?" I asked. "Maybe you could do cinnamon buns and donuts."

"One," said Nans.

"Then you should do a donut," Skylar said.

"But how could I possibly pick which of the donuts I'd submit? They're like my children. I love them all."

"Do your craziest one," said Sky. "Like the Everything donut."

The Everything donut is actually an invention of my cousin Lily. She's sort of a klutz, and one time she caused a tray of crumb-cake donuts to tip over onto a mixed tray of maple bacon and red velvet donuts that were side by side. The results turned out to be delicious, and they became the Everything donut.

I understood where Skylar was coming from, but I suddenly remembered what Ria had said the other night at Donut Dreams.

I nodded. "Yes. Or . . ."

Nans looked at me expectantly.

Ria had said that a glazed donut would tell her how good the donuts were, and not just the toppings.

"Or just do glazed," I said boldly.

Nans's eyes widened. "Glazed! That's a joke. That's not imaginative at all!"

But Skylar was nodding. "Yes. The glazed are awesome. When I bring donuts into school, they go first."

"It's what you're known for. It's the classic," I agreed, suddenly very sure of this idea.

Nans sighed heavily and surveyed the mess of the

kitchen. She grabbed a chunk of cinnamon bun and popped it into her mouth, chewing thoughtfully.

"But the cinnamon buns are so good," she said, sounding like a sad little kid.

She wiped her arm across her forehead and left a new streak of flour there.

"You could put them on the menu here and see how they do," I said. "People would pay top dollar for those babies!"

Nans looked so glum, I felt sorry for her.

Suddenly, Skylar climbed down from his stool, wet a paper towel with warm water, and walked over to Nans. He then proceeded to gently wipe the flour from her face.

Nans and I exchanged a surprised look when Sky went to toss the paper towel in the trash.

"Thank you, sweetheart. I must look a mess," said Nans. "And do you know what? I think you've grown!"

Sky shrugged, his moment of tenderness over. "Could I please have a grilled cheese for an after-school snack?"

"Sure, honey," said my grandmother. "Go get started on your homework and I'll bring it out."

Sky left the kitchen, and Nans and I smiled at

each other. "He's definitely grown about an inch. I knew he had to be putting all that food somewhere!" she said.

"It's sad my mom won't get to see him as he grows," I said, thinking of the out-of-date sketches in her studio.

"Oh, sweetheart," Nans said, gathering me into a floury hug. "I'm sure she's watching from somewhere. And she's very, very proud of you both!"

I pulled away and smiled at Nans.

"She'll be even prouder when you win the bake-off!" I teased.

"Oh, you!" said Nans, tweaking my nose.

Chapter Nine
Filling in the Pieces

The week passed quickly, with Casey and me treating each other carefully but pleasantly. I was looking forward to Saturday, when we'd be able to reconnect and have fun, just like old times.

Ria was also being very nice and seemed excited about our "study date."

I could see that progress was being made on her bakery each time I passed, and I was both eager and nervous to see inside on Saturday. Maybe I'd even get a sneak peek at what they were submitting to the bake-off!

The school was all abuzz with talk about the contest. Mr. Franklin had won one of the coveted bake-off slots, and my art class tried during both times we met to get him to tell us what he was going to make.

"Is it something chocolate?" asked Melanie.

Mr. Franklin just mimed zipping his lips and smiled.

"I know! It's a splatter cake, all decorated like that artist you showed us," I guessed.

"Jackson Pollock!" crowed Carmen.

"No, Mr. Franklin loves raspberry. Remember how he always has a raspberry granola bar?" Jamie grinned.

But Mr. Franklin would only smile and shrug and say, "Just wait until Sunday, people!"

With all the talk about the bake-off, I began to wonder if my advice to Nans had been wrong. Kids would come up to me and say, "What kind of donuts will you guys be making for the bake-off?"

And I wished I could surprise them and say, "Donuts? Why would you assume we'd be making donuts?"

But then I'd remember what Ria had said, and so I'd just copy Mr. Franklin, zipping my lips and pretending to throw away the key.

In my heart of hearts, I knew we should stick

with what made us great, what people loved us for.

But there was a part of me that wished Nans would throw caution to the wind and submit something crazy, like on *The Great British Baking Show*.

And people could say, "Wow, we didn't realize the Park was so gourmet! We never knew you had it in you! You should open a bakery!" and they'd forget all about the Rich Port Cakery.

❈   ❈   ❈   ❈   ❈

I worked Friday afternoon and it was slow; Saturday couldn't come fast enough. Then I worked the Saturday morning shift at Donut Dreams and it went super fast.

I'd brought my school bag along so I could go straight to Ria's shop afterward.

But as I changed out of my Dream Team T-shirt, I realized it had all come too fast: I was feeling very nervous. My hands were sweaty and I was shaky; my heart was even racing. I just didn't want to get to the Rich Port Cakery and find out it was going to blow us all away.

At ten minutes to twelve, I slowly came out of the staff bathroom, where I'd been changing. Grandpa was sitting at the front counter, chatting with Jenna, who was filling salt and pepper shakers.

"Hey, Grandpa! I'm heading out now. Going to do some detective work to check out the competition."

"And who would that be?" he asked, peering down at me over his half-moon glasses.

"The Salases' bakery!" *Duh,* I wanted to add, but didn't.

"Oh, please. They're not our competition. They're going to be good for our business. You wait and see!"

He shuffled the menus he was sorting and stacked them neatly in a pile.

"Okay, Grandpa! See you later!"

"Not if I see you first!"

He always says that, and it cracks him up, but the rest of us don't get it.

I smiled and Jenna and I exchanged an eye roll, and then I headed out. No more delays or excuses.

The Cakery was not too far away—a half a block along Main Street, and then one block ahead on Newtown Lane.

I looked through my phone—Casey was texting to ask what to pack for tonight, Jamie was asking about art homework, Kelsey was sending me her outfit choices for the bake-off. I was so distracted that I got to the cakery before I realized it.

The Salases had taken the brown craft paper off the windows since I'd passed by yesterday, and the windows looked really nice. I stepped up and peered inside.

The inside seemed to be finished too. I could see Ria and her family bustling around, laughing, calling to each other across the room.

The space was very unlike the Park or Donut Dreams. It felt very city-ish, or "urban" as Mr. Franklin would say—the colors were all black and red with brass highlights.

The back wall had white subway tiles on it and brass railings along the counter like a bar. There were brass light fixtures on the ceiling and walls, with small glass bulbs that were see-through and old-fashioned but modern and cool-looking at the same time.

The floor was tiled in little black-and-white designs, and there was a big, brightly lit bakery case along one wall and small café tables and chairs along the other wall.

The whole place felt like it belonged in downtown Chicago, in a good way.

Suddenly, Ria spotted me and began waving me in.

I took a deep breath and pushed open the front door, with its handsome brass handle.

"Hey, Lindsay!" called Ria. "Come in for your tour!"

Mr. and Mrs. Salas popped their heads out from the back room. They were both wearing comfortable clothes—Mr. Salas held a paintbrush, while Mrs. Salas, a cleaning cloth in her hand, had her hair tied up in a cool bandanna.

"Lindsay! Hi!" they both called to me.

I waved and smiled. They really were so friendly.

Luis came darting out of the back and right to my side.

"I made you a dessert!" he said proudly, with a gap-toothed grin.

"You did?!" I bent down so I was closer to his size. "What is it?" I asked.

He smiled. "It's a surprise!" he said and took off again.

Ria rolled her eyes. "You're his new best friend, ever since the Oreo donut. Also, I gave him the extra glazed donut that you gave me and he liked that even better! Go figure."

"The way to a boy's heart is though his stomach," I said with a laugh. "At least in my family."

"That is the truth! Here, put your stuff down and I'll show you around."

Ria led me over to one of the cute bistro tables and I set my bag down on the chair next to it.

"Everything is so pretty and stylish and fresh!" I said, spinning in place to take it all in.

I had a smile plastered to my face because what I really felt was dismay for Donut Dreams and the Park View Table. They were going to seem overly familiar and tired compared to this shiny new place.

"Thanks," said Ria, bursting with pride. "My parents have been working so hard. I'm really excited for them. It's a dream come true. Our old neighborhood in Chicago had gotten kind of dangerous with crime in the city lately, and they were so happy to get us out here into the fresh air with nice people and safe streets."

"Wait, what?"

My grandparents hadn't hinted at this at all.

Ria nodded and lowered her voice. "My parents don't know I overhead this, but a shop up the street from our cake shop was robbed a couple of months back. That's why they finally made this move—also why they did it at such a weird time of year. They were just like, 'Let's go. Now.'"

Ria's eyes were big and serious.

I let out the breath I'd been holding. "Wow. That is so scary. I'm really sorry."

I felt terrible. If I'd known that Ria's family had been escaping danger in the city, I'd have been a whole lot more welcoming sooner.

But Ria's eyes were dancing again. "Actually, I'm happy about it. I love Bellgrove. It's a town like I've always dreamed of. My grandparents might move out here next summer too. And maybe even some of my cousins, which would be awesome."

"Be careful what you wish for!" I said with a laugh.

Ria smiled. "You don't know how lucky you are, with Kelsey and Molly in your actual grade at school. It's so cool. I'd give anything for my cousin Laura to be in my class!"

"Then I hope it happens," I said.

"Thanks," Ria said. "Come on, I'll show you around."

We went all around the main room, my mind

still reeling from the news of their escape as Ria showed me all the up-to-date appliances and how the bakery case worked, and the gleaming red-and-brass cappuccino machine.

"Puerto Rico was famous for its coffee for centuries. Then they slowed down, but lately farmers there have been getting back into small-batch boutique coffee," said Ria with a smile. "My parents are obsessed, and they'll only be serving Puerto Rican coffee. Come see the kitchen."

In the back, the kitchen was a lot like the one at the Park, only smaller. Ria's mom was cleaning the inside of the huge walk-in fridge where the special-order cakes would go, and she popped out to chat with us a for a minute.

"Everything looks great!" I said. "You could open tomorrow!"

She smiled. "Thanks. I think we're aiming for Tuesday. We'll get through the bake-off tomorrow and take a day to clean up, and then we're live!"

"Cool," I said.

I was dying to know what they were making for the bake-off but figured it would be unsportsmanlike to ask.

Luis popped into the kitchen and said, "Mamí, is now the time?"

"Sure, *mi amor*. Go ahead."

He grinned and walked over to a large refrigerator and yanked the handle down to open it. It was the size of a vault, and bright white light spilled out from inside.

Carefully, Luis withdrew a platter covered by a glass dome and brought it to the high-top counter we were gathered around. He lifted the glass dome off the platter and said, "Ta-da!"

It looked like a cheesecake—a large, round, pale pudding of some sort, with a thick layer of caramel on top.

"Wow!" I breathed in the scent of toasted sugar. "It's beautiful! It even smells amazing. What is it?"

"Have some!" he said. "Try it! It's called flan!"

Ria said, "She needs a knife and a plate, silly."

But their mom was one step ahead. She had a small stack of plates and a cake server.

"Luis, baby, grab some forks from the drawer, please."

He dashed off as she sliced the flan into thick, wobbly slices and plated one for each of us.

Once everyone was served, I took a forkful and lifted it to my mouth. The scent of cream and vanilla, along with the caramelized-sugar smell of the topping, teased my nose and set my mouth to watering. I put the bite in my mouth and was rewarded by an intense flavor burst of many different and wonderful elements.

The flan was creamy like vanilla pudding, but the vanilla was rich and distinct from the cream taste. There was a whisper of vanilla bean, and then the thick, chewy layer of caramel on top was in contrast to the cool cream that melted in my mouth.

It was incredible.

"Oh my goodness!" I cried when I could speak again. "This is insane! It's like nothing I've ever had before. What's it called again?" I jammed another bite in my mouth.

"Flan!" said Luis, his cheek flecked with cream. "I helped make it!"

"Luis, you are an amazing baker!" I said.

He grinned.

"Is this a Puerto Rican specialty?" I asked, hoovering it down.

"Yes," said Mrs. Salas. "Actually, it's a really ancient

dessert from Rome that traveled the world. Spain popularized it and brought it to the Americas, and it's really big in Puerto Rico, with all kinds of variations. This is the classic version."

"I love it. What are the other kinds of desserts you'll have here?"

Mrs. Salas began describing their specialties. "*Pastelitos*, which are little puff pastries with sweet jam fillings; *arroz con leche*, which is rice pudding with cinnamon; *tembleque*, which is like coconut cream Jell-O; *besitos de coco*, which are coconut 'kisses,' like shredded coconut drop cookies."

"Oh, I had one of those when you brought them to school. They're amazing!" I said to Ria.

Her mom beamed and continued, "We'll have pineapple rum cake, and *quesitos*, which are little cigar-shaped cream-and-jam-filled pastries. . . ."

"Those are my favorites!" said Ria. "Yum!"

"And, of course, we'll have all kinds of cake!" said Mrs. Salas with a smile.

"Gosh, it all sounds awesome. I'm so excited to try everything!"

Nans had been right: everything was totally different from what we sell at Donut Dreams or the

Park. Even their coffee would be different. I was honestly looking forward to experiencing all these specialties.

I felt giddy with relief.

"'Tastes just like fancy restaurant cooking!' That's what we say in our family when we eat our own cooking."

The Salases all laughed.

"That's so funny. We do the same thing, but we say, 'You know, you could be a professional!'" said Mrs. Salas.

"Okay, professional, should we get to work?" asked Ria with a smile.

"Sure," I said.

I stashed my plate and fork in the industrial dishwasher—just like the one we have at the Park— and we set out our supplies.

"Just don't make too much of a mess, *mija*," said Mrs. Salas to Ria.

"Okay, Mamí, we won't. Lindsay's used to restaurant cleanup anyway!" she called.

Ria and I smiled at each other, and we began to work.

We found a butter cookie recipe online that we

could tweak, and we set to work making half batches of it with baking soda or baking powder.

While the cookies baked, we searched the Internet and some standard cookbooks of Mrs. Salas's for information on the differences between baking soda and baking powder and worked on our thesis and an outline for the report.

I was pleasantly surprised to see how well Ria and I worked together.

We were mostly quiet while researching, and we both got right down to our tasks. We chatted easily while we were measuring and mixing, and then refocused again.

Ria was a great listener and asked thoughtful questions. She was also really smart and calm. This was a different Ria than the social butterfly I'd been seeing at school.

Mrs. Salas came through once in a while and answered questions for us. She was obviously a very accomplished baker; she'd even been to cooking school. Her information really helped us shape our project.

After three hours of straight work, Ria and I felt we had the research we needed to complete the project. We'd meet after school this week and figure out who would write up which parts, and then we'd bake the cookie samples to bring in.

Mrs. Salas passed back through as we dried the final mixing bowl.

"Maria, *mi amor*, is there any chance you'd help me with the flower planters outside? I want to get those done this afternoon. It makes me sad to see them empty. I've got some mums in the back of the truck."

It was only four o'clock, and I still had some time before Casey was due at my house.

"I'll help too!" I offered.

"Oh, Lindsay, you are a peach. Thanks!"

Ria and I went out the back to the Salases' pickup truck and began unloading the pots of mums and the heavy bags of potting soil.

The four low rectangular black planters were lined up in a row. We needed to fill the planters with chunks of Styrofoam to take up space, then pour in some soil, carefully shake the plants out of their containers, and neatly nestle them into the planters. Then we'd fill in with the extra soil and carry the planters to the front of the store.

Mrs. Salas was there to help too, and Mr. Salas would help carry the planters afterward.

Getting my hands in the soil felt just like baking, and the fresh, earthy smell reminded me of my mom. I'd always hang around with her while she worked in her garden when I was little.

I wished I had done it more, because she always invited me to help. But I found I remembered more than I would have thought.

"Do you have a little fertilizer we can sprinkle in before we add the plants?" I asked Mrs. Salas.

She stood up and smiled broadly. "We have a gardener!" she cheered. "Yes, I do, Lindsay! Thank you for reminding me. It's in the front seat."

She came back with a small bag and handed it to me gingerly.

"It smells awful," she cautioned.

"I know," I said with a smile.

I ripped a corner of the bag and lightly sprinkled it along the dirt in all four planters.

"How did you learn about gardening?" asked Mrs. Salas, as she shook the mums out of their plastic pots one by one.

"My mom was obsessed with flowers, and she

had a cutting garden. She used to do these huge arrangements and drop them off."

Mrs. Salas smacked her forehead. "Of course! Casey has told us all about her and how wonderful she was. I'm so sorry that part slipped my mind! 'Flowerbombing'! What fun. I'm crazy about flowers too. Your mom and I would have had a ton to talk about."

While a year ago this conversation might have made me super sad, today it actually made me happy.

"I bet you two would have been great friends!" I said, and I meant it.

"I am sure we would have. I'm looking forward to learning more about her, and I'm so glad I'll get to know you, too," said Mrs. Salas. "What are you doing with her garden now?"

"Well, it's funny you should mention it," I said, and began to fill her in.

Chapter Ten
New Beginnings

My afternoon at the Rich Port Cakery with the Salas family was amazing. I felt like Ria and I really became friends, and I also felt close to her whole family at the end. I could see how Casey had warmed to them so easily.

I was happy I'd had the opportunity to help them a little bit by planting the planters, and I was pleased to see my handiwork out front when I passed by later.

My detective report to my grandpa would have been: *The Salas family is super nice and their cakery is going to be a huge success.* And I wasn't upset or worried about it at all anymore.

Ria's mom had promised to bring me her seed and flower nursery catalogs to look over, and she said

I should flag the flowers and plants I liked and then she'd help me make a plan for spring planting.

I was so excited. I would update my mom's garden and make sure it had tons of flowers in all different colors—crazy and wild and bursting with life, with plenty of blue flowers mixed in. No plain old regimented, over-pruned, one-color garden for me! I knew my mom would have loved to see me getting into it.

Casey arrived that night at six on the dot. My dad and Skylar were out at a friend of Sky's laser tag birthday, so we had the house to ourselves. We made French bread pizzas for dinner, and for dessert we warmed up Nans's cinnamon buns.

Casey showed me the new art photography Instagram account that her mom let her start. It was private for now, but Casey said her mom had promised to reevaluate it in six months, and if Casey kept all identifying details out of her posts, her mom might let her make it public so she could gain followers with hashtags.

I scrolled through all her artsy photos and was blown away.

"Wow, Case, these are amazing!" I said.

She had some sensational action photos of our friends playing sports, but she'd take close-ups of, like, a foot in midair, or a hockey stick in a hand, and she'd saturate the colors and blur the background so everything looked hyper-real. The photos were kind of edgy and really well composed.

"Mr. Franklin would be so proud!" I said. "Look at how you use the negative space! And the color palette is so vivid. And the contrasting textures just make it so rich. . . ."

I felt Casey staring at me. "What?" I said.

Her jaw was open. "You could be a professional art critic!" she said. "How do you know all this terminology?"

I shrugged. "I don't know. Just from listening to my mom over the years, I guess. Then Mr. Franklin uses some of it, so it just triggers the rest. It's all coming back to me!" I joked.

"Well, you've got a future in art, one way or another," said Casey.

Her compliments made me glow inside. I felt warm and happy and connected to both Casey and my mom right then.

I was also really proud of Casey and a little

relieved to see that she was actually a really good photographer.

I felt guilty that I had doubted her new passion; it had seemed to come out of nowhere, but maybe I just hadn't been paying enough attention to her interests for a long time.

I thought about the advice Nans had given me, and now was the perfect time to acknowledge my own shortcomings as a friend.

"Casey, I just wanted to say, I know I'm not always the greatest friend. I can be pretty wrapped up in my own stuff and not paying close attention to you. And I also know that the thing with my mom dying has been a lot for you, too, as my friend and also because . . . well . . . you lost her too."

Casey's eyes welled up and she dove at me for a hug. "That is so sweet, Lindsay. Thank you!"

She squeezed me so hard, and then she let go and there were tears on her cheeks.

"I really do miss your mom so much, but I feel like I can't complain about it to you because, OMG, you lost your *mom*! I just lost my friend's mom, and my mom's friend," she said.

"She was your friend too, Casey. And she would

have been so happy to see you becoming an artist, and so proud of you. I know it in my heart."

Casey squeezed me again. "I bet my mom would have even let her follow me on Instagram!" she joked. She pulled away. "And you *are* a great friend. You've just had a lot going on."

"But I know you cover for me and stuff, and try to help me, like with new friends and everything, and I really appreciate it. You're the best flower in my garden!" I said.

"And you're the best one in mine, whatever that means!"

We hugged it out again and then carried on with our fun sleepover.

☀ ☀ ☀ ☀ ☀

The next morning we slept until ten o'clock, and when we wandered downstairs my dad said, "I was just about to get you up. We've got some gardening to do this morning, and then it's bake-off time and Nans needs our help transporting some things to the tent in town!"

"Ooh, I am so excited, Mr. Cooper!" said Casey. "I wonder who's going to win!"

"If I know my mother," said my dad with a wink, "she'll figure out a way for everyone to win!"

We had a quick breakfast—just some cereal—and then we set off for the garden, with Casey trailing along behind to help.

"It would make me feel close to your mom," she had offered.

I knew what she meant. I'd felt the same way yesterday digging in the dirt with Ria and her mom.

"I'd be thrilled if you stayed!" I said with a huge smile.

My dad had bought mulch, and we worked pulling weeds and trimming down any dead areas on the plants, which was a lot.

Soon we had a neat-looking bed of small, nubby plants, well-watered and surrounded by fragrant pine mulch.

"What's the mulch for? To keep them warm?" asked Casey.

"Believe it or not, it's to keep them cold, once the ground freezes. If they warm up too soon, they'll sprout too early and then they can die," I told her.

"Huh. Learn something new every day," said Casey. "And what about the plants that are left?"

Suddenly, a car horn tooted and the Salases' pickup truck pulled into our driveway.

Casey and I stood up and brushed off our hands, then jogged over to the truck, where Ria was already stepping out. Her mom was behind the wheel.

"Hi, girls! I have some extra burlap from my garden at the house and I wanted to drop it off for you on our way by. Lindsay, honey, you'll want to wrap any plant that's more than a foot tall, so they don't get crushed by snow this winter. Use some of the wooden stakes I've included to help keep the plant upright. Then tie it off with the ball of twine. Ria's got it all for you. Call us if you have any trouble with it," Mrs. Salas said.

Ria came around from the back of the truck with a cardboard box. Inside were a few dozen stakes, the twine, and a big roll of burlap. On top were three thick seed catalogs.

"Wow, Mrs. Salas! This is so nice of you!"

My dad had reached the truck and was smiling at my side. "Thanks so much, Serena," he said. "I really appreciate it!"

Mrs. Salas nodded and put the truck in reverse. "We can't begin to thank the Cooper family for all the help and support you've given us. My only regret is that I didn't get to know your mom, Lindsay. This is my way of making friends with her. Good luck with the garden, and we'll see you all at the bake-off!"

She backed the truck out as we called our thank-yous after her.

"Wow. That is just so nice!" I said, waving at Ria.

"They're wonderful people," said my dad. "Grandpa was right. We're lucky to have them here in Bellgrove."

"Yes," I agreed, meaning it wholeheartedly. "And they make great desserts!"

❀ ❀ ❀ ❀ ❀

After we'd tucked the garden in for the winter, Casey called her mom to let her know she'd head straight to town with us. We swung by the Park, which was bustling with diners and, of course, my family members getting ready for the bake-off.

By twelve thirty, my grandpa's truck was loaded with folding tables, chairs, platters, boxes of napkins and more, and my dad was behind the wheel.

We eased down the dirt path along the side of the town park and pulled up to the tent to unload. The events would start at two o'clock, so we had time to set up and then grab some lunch at the restaurant.

Ria came running over to say hi. Her parents were struggling to get some tables set up, so my dad sent over my cousin Rich and my uncle Charlie to help them. All the other bakers—including the bake-off contestants—were setting up their tables and beginning to lay out their wares. The tent smelled incredible and the vibe was pure sugar-high.

After we set up our tables and chairs and laid out the platters, Casey and I did a lap to see if we could size up the competition.

Most people hadn't set out their food yet, so we just greeted everyone and wandered around until we got back to Ria's table. They were good to go now, thanks to my family's help, and were also going to wait until the last minute to bring out their goodies.

There was a central table selling food tickets. The way it worked was, you could buy as many tickets as you liked, and each vendor would give you one portion of any of their items for one ticket.

We each purchased a bunch of tickets and agreed to share the things we bought—that way we could try everything!

Luckily, it was a beautiful fall day: blue sky, warm sun, and a cool breeze. The town had put out hay bales all around the lawn outside the tent and in front of the stage where the bands would perform. It looked like an old-fashioned hoedown.

※ ※ ※ ※ ※

At opening time, the bakers began lifting covers off trays and having family members arrive with their last-minute baked goods—keeping them as fresh as possible until the final moment.

There was one giant table that had been taped in a grid, with each square numbered. The bake-off contestants had to each put their item in their assigned square, and the judging would begin at three o'clock.

We stood by the table, watching the bake-off contestants arrive, bearing their items with pride, while Casey snapped photos of everyone and their desserts.

Nans came with a platter of the most perfect-looking glazed donuts you ever saw. I mean, I can eat as many donuts as I want every day, so I shouldn't have even cared, but these made my mouth water. They were double-dipped, and the glaze was shiny and crinkly over the crisp brown donuts. Perfection.

I was so proud of her and my whole family, and extra pleased that she had taken advice from me and Skylar on what to bake.

Mr. Franklin brought raspberry cream-cheese crumble bars that were magazine-worthy. He grinned sheepishly when Jamie teased him about being predictable.

Ria nudged me as she watched Jamie. "He's cute," she said.

"Really?" I tipped my head. "I never thought of him like that," I admitted.

"And I think he likes you. Look how he keeps looking at you to see if you're liking his jokes." She nodded knowledgeably, but I just rolled my eyes.

"Whatever," I said.

I was not interested in Jamie like that, but it was nice to have Ria think he was interested in me.

And right then, Mrs. Salas arrived with a platter of flan! It looked even more beautiful than the one from yesterday and had a flurry of sea salt flakes scattered across the top.

Luis skipped along behind her, clapping his hands in excitement.

I turned to Ria. "Flan!" I said. "Yay!"

"She had a really hard time deciding what to make, but in the end she felt that flan was a classic, and her specialty, and that it would really stand out. I said it would be a good introduction to all our specialty Puerto Rican sweets, and that's what clinched it. She's calling it Puerto Rican Gold."

Just like us and our glazed donuts, I thought.

"Puerto Rican Gold! Great name!" enthused Casey.

"And true!" I added.

After that, Ria and Casey and I meandered around, trying as many sweets as possible while Casey snapped tons of photos and Jamie trailed around behind us.

There was an amazing range of treats to sample: peanut butter brownies, salted caramel chocolate chip cookies, orange blossom angel food cake, butterscotch pudding, bacon-caramel cupcakes, red velvet rainbow cakes, painted sugar cookies, cheesecakes, raspberry linzer torte cookies, gingersnaps, lemon squares, pink strawberry shortcake cake pops, Saint Louis butter cake, grasshopper pie, you name it!

Ready, Set, Bake!

Desserts were sticky, chewy, crunchy, warm, chilled, salty-sweet, tart, syrupy—every good adjective you could think of.

We were practically sick by the time the judging started.

At exactly three o'clock, the mayor gathered everyone to the bake-off table. She stood behind it on a small step with all the judges (including Casey's mom) behind her. She called the crowd to order and began to speak.

"I'd like to welcome you all to our first annual Bellgrove Bake Sale and Bake-Off! All of our proceeds are going to the ongoing cause of Puerto Rican hurricane relief—the mess is still real there, folks, so please do your best to spend, spend, spend today, and we'll get those funds down to the schools and shelters there," she said.

She paused before she continued. "First of all, I'd like to thank our founding co-chairs, Jane Cooper and Serena Salas. These two dynamos organized this whole event in just a week, and we are all grateful to them for their energy, style, and inclusiveness. Let's give them a big hand!"

Nans and Mrs. Salas stepped forward with their

arms around each other and waved to the crowd with wide smiles while Casey snapped photo after photo.

The mayor continued. "Next, I'd like to thank all the volunteers who made today possible, as well as all the participants. Bellgrove has some of the most talented bakers in the world, it seems, and I was honored to participate as a judge! I'd like to go through the winners now. . . ."

Everyone hooted and hollered and clapped, and the mayor began reading the awards.

Just as my dad had predicted, there was no one overall winner of the bake-off. Instead, there were different categories, and everything came in first in its category.

I felt a little let down—I had really wanted our donuts to win "Best in Show," but I had also desperately not wanted to get beaten by the Salas family, no matter how much I had grown to like them and their new shop.

The categories were clever, though, and all the awards made people feel good, so I guess it was worth it in the end.

Donut Dreams won "Best Dunking Treat." The Rich Port Cakery's Puerto Rican Gold flan won

"International Miracle." Mr. Franklin's crumble bars won "Most Delicious Portable Treat." And so on.

"I guess there really isn't a way to say what's the absolute best treat of all," I said to Ria and Casey after it was all over. "Everyone's tastes are so different."

Casey agreed. "And you want different types of treats at different times of day. . . ."

"Or after eating different kinds of food," Ria said.

"It's all about the mix," I summed it up. "Everyone brings something different to the table and it's all good. There's room for everyone."

"Exactly," said Casey.

"I wonder what flan-filled donuts would taste like?" I said.

"Oooh!" Casey said. "Tell Nans that idea!"

"I think I will!" I replied, smiling at the thought.

※　※　※　※　※

On Monday morning I came downstairs to find four big boxes of donuts waiting for me.

Nans was standing there drinking a big cup of coffee, and she grinned when I came in.

"I brought these donuts for you to give away at school today!" she announced brightly.

"Nans! It's not even my birthday! Aunt Mel's gonna kill you!" I said.

I peeked inside: a dozen glazed, a dozen cinnamon, two dozen mixed.

"I know. I just thought you seemed like you needed a lift."

I played it cool, but I was touched.

"Maybe. Thanks. These are awesome, and you know who will be most excited?"

We locked eyes and laughed as we singsonged her name together: "Casey!"

❈   ❈   ❈   ❈   ❈

The Rich Port Cakery opened Tuesday morning with great fanfare. I arrived after school and the place was jammed.

Nans had taken me to the florist, where I filled a brass watering can with an explosion of flowers to give to the Salas family for good luck.

I made sure to include red and gold flowers to go along with their decor, but I also snuck in a couple of cornflower-blue ones, so my mom could be there in spirit.

"It's a flowerbomb!" said Mrs. Salas. "Just like your

mom used to make! I love it. Thank you so much, *mi amor.*" She gave me a squeeze.

I'd written a good luck card to go along with the flowerbomb too, and I included a doodle on the front of the card. Ria opened it when I presented the flowers to her and her mom.

"Lindsay, this drawing is really good!" said Ria, showing her mom my doodle. "You could sell these!"

It was a drawing of a seedling just popping up from the dirt with the caption, *Here's to new beginnings!*

I liked that it represented a few different beginnings—the cakery and our new friendship, not to mention Mrs. Salas's and my shared love of gardening.

"Thanks," I said to Ria. "I might do that. I know a place that carries cards like this."

"Come get something to eat!" she said, pulling me by the arm to the counter.

The array of pastries and confections was staggering, and they were flying off the counter as people ordered snacks for now and desserts to take home.

But suddenly, I spotted something that took my breath away. Near the center of the counter was a platter of perfectly glazed donuts. My heart lurched in my chest. So they *were* competing with us!

Ria saw me spot the donuts and said, "Oh, it's so cute, your grandparents are going to carry our desserts at the restaurant, and my parents are going to offer your donuts here. We're all doubling our exposure to the world! Look at the little sign Casey made!"

Next to the donut platter was an incredibly realistic drawing of a donut on a plate in a small frame. Underneath the picture, she had beautifully hand-lettered, *Donuts for All by Donut Dreams*.

"I love it! There's something old and something new," I said, gesturing at the Puerto Rican desserts and then at the donuts.

"Something borrowed, and something blue!" said Ria, gesturing at the watering can and the blue flowers tucked inside.

"Donuts and flan: a match made in heaven!" I said.

To new beginnings! I thought, and my heart was full.

Still Hungry?
Here's a taste of the sixth book in the

series, **Ready to Roll!**

Chapter One
Rain or Shine

It had been raining buckets of hard, cold rain nonstop all week. There were puddles everywhere and everyone was in a sour mood, including me. Nothing had gone really, really wrong, but it just seemed like nothing was going right, either.

Usually, Molly and I walk home after school, but Dad had been picking us up all week so we wouldn't get drenched. Even though he always parked in the same place, when Dad saw us he blinked his lights twice so we'd know which car was his. It was a little embarrassing since we were in middle school now and we knew how to find our dad, but it was also a little comforting.

I darted into the car and slammed the door shut. Molly opened the door on the other side and jumped in.

"Ugh!" Molly groaned, getting her umbrella caught in the frame of the door.

"Molly, shut the door!" I yelled.

The rain was coming in sideways and the whole seat was getting wet.

"I'm trying!" yelled Molly as she threw the umbrella across the back of the car, splattering water everywhere.

Dad sighed and shook his head.

"Hello, you two balls of sunshine!" he said cheerily. "Everyone have a good day?"

"It was okay," I said and sighed. "Not great."

"I hate this rain," said Molly. "We had PE inside. And soccer practice is indoors this week."

"The trees and the plants and the lakes like the water," said Dad, pulling out of the parking lot.

Dad always believed in seeing the upside of things.

We were all quiet on the way home. The windshield wipers went back and forth furiously and the rain slammed into the car.

Then Dad's phone dinged, and I glanced at it.

"It's from Mom," I said, grabbing it.

"Hey!" said Dad. "That's my phone, not yours. And I'm driving!"

Then my phone dinged. "Okay," I said. "Now it's Mom on my phone."

Molly's phone dinged too.

"What's up?" asked Dad, sounding a little worried.

"Nans can't pick up Lindsay," I said, reading my screen.

My grandmother, whom I call Nans, usually picked up my cousin Lindsay after school.

"Tell Mom we've got it," said Dad, turning around the block and pulling back into the school lot.

The line of cars had already left, even in that short time, so we drove right up to the entrance. Lindsay was waiting there with her huge knapsack and a big pink umbrella with rainbows all over it.

I felt bad because she was the last one waiting, alone. Her mom had died a few years ago, and since then the whole family has pitched in to help Uncle Mike, Lindsay, and her younger brother, Skylar. Nans and Grandpa live really close by, so there's always someone around, but still, it's times like these that it feels like she's missing someone.

Dad flicked the lights at Lindsay.

"Here we are," he called, even though she couldn't hear him from outside the car.

I knew then that Dad was thinking the same thing I was. I looked over at him and smiled.

Lindsay opened the door and slid in. "Thanks Uncle Chris," she said. "Ugh, there's a puddle on this seat."

"Molly did it," I said.

"It was an accident," Molly said dramatically.

"Oh, that's right, Molly had an accident," I said. "On the seat." I started to giggle.

"What kind of accident?" Lindsay asked mischievously.

"You know what kind," I said, turning around.

"You are kidding!" said Molly. "Stop taunting me!"

"Molly, you said you had an accident," I said.

"Not that kind of accident!" Molly yelled.

"Girls, I am trying to drive a car in the middle of a rainstorm," Dad said, even though he was trying not to laugh.

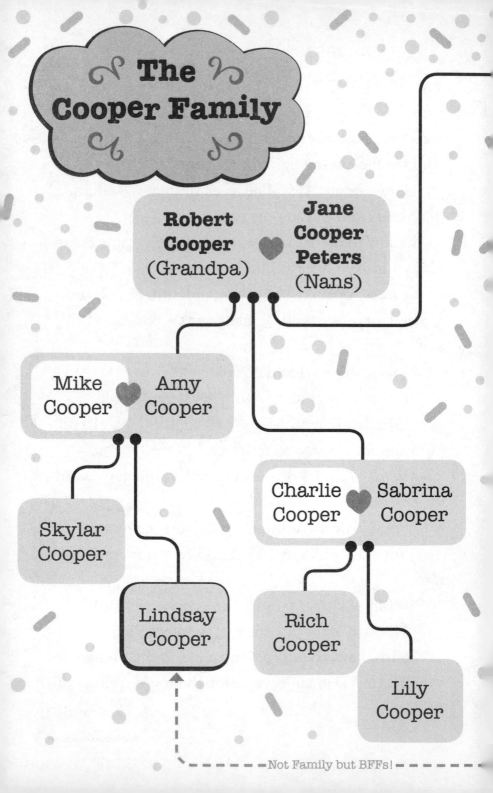

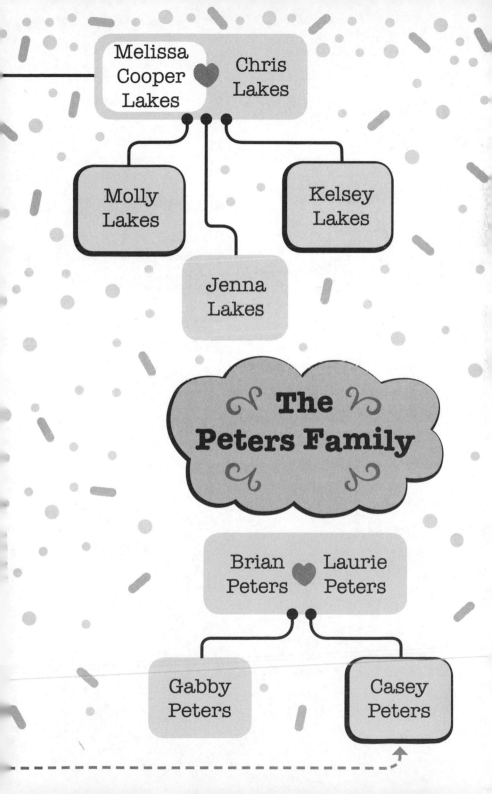